Dancing at the Victory Café

LEAH FLEMING

**SIMON &
SCHUSTER**

London · New York · Sydney · Toronto · New Delhi

A CBS COMPANY

First published in Great Britain by Coronet, an imprint of Hodder & Stoughton, 1995
This paperback first published by Simon & Schuster UK Ltd, 2016
A CBS Company

1 3 5 7 9 10 8 6 4 2

Simon & Schuster UK Ltd
1st Floor
222 Gray's Inn Road
London WC1X 8HB

www.simonandschuster.co.uk

Simon & Schuster Australia, Sydney
Simon & Schuster India, New Delhi

A CIP catalogue record for this book is available from the British Library

Paperback ISBN: 978-1-4711-5912-1
eBook ISBN: 978-1-4711-5914-5

Typeset in the UK by Hewer Text UK Ltd, Edinburgh
Printed and bound in Great Britain by CPI Group (UK) Ltd, Croydon, CR0 4YY

MIX
Paper from
responsible sources
FSC® C020471

In loving memory of my parents,
Alex and Helen Fleming

If you love a person, you want them to be happy, not take them like butter and spread them thinly over your own bread to make it more palatable for yourself.

From *Nella Last's Wartime Diary*
(Mass Observation Unit)

Author's Note

This is a reissue of my first novel: *Dancing at the Victory Café*, which was published under my original name, Helene Wiggin, in 1995 to commemorate the fiftieth anniversary of the ending of the Second World War. Now that I am better known as Leah Fleming, I'm keeping life simple by sticking to that name.

The events and characters in this story are entirely fictitious and any mistakes in locations or dates are entirely my own. However, running a café in a market square for several years gave me many useful experiences to share in this story.

I am indebted to friends and relatives for wartime stories and recipes, especially the late Vivien Dewes, who first sparked my interest in wartime Lichfield. I have used the late Marguerite Patten's *Till We Eat Again* for information on the Kitchen Front.

I would like to thank my agent, Judith Murdoch who saw the potential in a raw piece of writing and encouraged me to polish it into something publishable. I would like to thank Joanne Dickinson and the team at Simon and Schuster for the lovely new cover.

I salute the '*loyal and ancient city of Lichfield*' for encouraging new writers with the former Lichfield Prize for which I was short-listed in 1993. I owe my writing career to the boost of confidence this gave me. Finally, as always, I thank David and my family for giving me the time and encouragement to write this story.

Leah

Contents

Friday Evening

The letter fell from her grasp, half open on the rug, like butterfly wings. Isobel Morton gazed out of her cottage window, tucked in an alley behind the Cathedral Close, to watch blue tits pecking mortar from the window frame. The wind rattled through the ancient building. She could feel the draught of winter on cheeks as thin as tissue paper; she sighed as her denim eyes, faded tearless, re-examined the pink notepaper.

Dear Mrs Morton,

    I saw your wartime cookery article in a magazine recently and just had to write to you with a belated, hello! It brought back such memories of our time together in the café.

    I shall take the liberty of calling to see you on Sunday afternoon.

    Never go back they say, but I am curious. It is time to tread the hard road of broken dreams, back to Lichfield, the city of my sorrow.

Yours sincerely,
(You will remember me as)
Dorrie Goodman

Isobel shook her head. 'It's come at last as I knew it must: the final demand note, fifty years too late. Just when I'd decided to slip away quietly with no fuss. I'm too tired for the song and dance routine she will want to perform. The day of reckoning is upon you, old girl, so dust down the Purchase Ledger and pay your dues.'

Already, memories were chipping in her head like woodpeckers hidden in a dark tree, hammering into the soul. *Where do I begin? Where were the seeds of love first sown?* Back, of course, in the spring of 1943, with the birth of the Victory Café.

1
VICTORY CAFÉ

<u>Menu</u>

Harvest Broth

Jugged Hare with Gamechips and Vegetables

Belle's Bread and Butter Pudding or Apple Pie and Custard

March 1943

'My dear, your hymen is holding up the works,' says the doctor with a torch on his head, like a miner peering down into a pit. He stretches and twists her insides like tough elastic. 'That's better. Now just you get that husband of yours to do his duty and you'll be back in no time, complaining of morning sickness!'

In four years of marriage, Belle Morton's husband had never managed to do his duty. She was sure nothing would change that state of affairs. 'It's not that easy, Doctor,' she stammers, as she mops up the blood between her legs. 'We, er . . . Dennis, can't seem to . . . to do anything.'

'Nonsense, young lady, a few whiskies . . . a bit of feminine encouragement.' It is the doctor's turn now to falter at specifics. 'Dennis Morton's a sensitive sort of chap and being in the forces isn't easy for a fastidious man . . . Just you relax. Let nature take its course. That'll be all.'

The doctor washes his hands. Belle adjusts her skirt and stockings. Her husband rarely comes home and when he does, he will down his spirits, flop to the far end of the double bed and rasp away the night with hearty snores. It is his mother who sits, like Madame Defarge, in the waiting room, knitting scarves not bootees, assuming the absence of offspring to be entirely the fault of a careless wife.

'We are hoping for a tribe of Mortons to see the Leather Works into the next century. His father was one of six sons. England expects, Isobel dear,' she hints, sniffing with a delicacy which restrains further comment.

Belle also expected more from the shy Works Manager, with his Leslie Howard good looks, expected more than a kiss and a cuddle on their wedding night, on their honeymoon in France and during the four dreary years of this wartime marriage.

Now her life is at a standstill, like Mona the Morris Eight tourer, sitting on bricks in the garage of their bungalow. The house has withstood the worst of the Birmingham blitz, ten miles away, but the marriage is shot to pieces. Belle adjusts her smile to face the inquisition on the other side of the door.

'Well? What does he say?'

'He thinks a change will do me good,' she lies.

'You know you can help out at the works any time, plenty of bookkeeping to keep you out of mischief,' her mother in law replies.

'I'd prefer to do something on my own, use my canteen training, catering perhaps.'

'I'm sure our Dennis would not want you mixing with roughnecks in a N.A.A.F.I. canteen. You're a Morton now. What would people think!'

'The Civic restaurant needs volunteers or the W.V.S. I don't do enough,' Belle continues.

'Don't you think you should stay close at hand for Dennis? His furlough is so unpredictable. If we're ever going to have our grandchild, you'll need to rest at your age. Thirty-five is cutting it a bit fine.' The gauntlet drops with a thud.

'I shouldn't bank on that, Mrs Morton.' The challenge is accepted.

'What do you mean? The doctor says you are A1, doesn't he?'

'Oh, yes, but it's not me with the problem, actually!'

'And just what does that mean?'

'I'd rather not say.'

'Are you suggesting that there is something wrong with our Dennis? He's fit enough to be in the forces, which is more than you are!' The hackles are rising.

'Yes, I know, but this is slightly different.'

'I don't like the tone of your remarks, Isobel. War is strenuous work. It separates a lot of couples but I don't see a shortage of bulging prams on the High Street. Explain yourself!'

'Not here, mother, another time.' Belle edges to the door. 'I do need a change, another outlet for my energies. Firewatching is not enough!'

'I hope you are not going to end up one of these soldiers' pickups. That's what happens to bored housewives with too much time and very little sense!' The woman stabs her needles into the ball of wool.

'How dare you! Only a warped mind would suggest such a thing. No wonder your precious son can't make a woman of me, can't do his duty by me. If we carry on much longer like this, it'll be an annulment, I'll be entitled to, not divorce!' Belle's blue eyes flash, hard as diamonds but the tears are welling fast.

'Don't make an exhibition of yourself, lady,' whispers the older woman. 'It could be said that a self-educated cook, who has too many opinions for her own good and jumped up notions, at that, might not encourage the passion in any man. I always told our Dennis he was a fool to pick a chainforger's daughter, when he could have had the cream of the local crop. You two were never suited.'

'Don't you think that is for us to decide? Instead of interfering at every turn. I've had enough of your opinions to last me a lifetime. There's more to life than providing heirs for Morton's Leather Works and I mean to find some.'

'And I shall be writing to Dennis, to tell him what an ungrateful wife he's lumbered with. Don't expect us to fund your selfish schemes. You go and suit yourself!'

'I certainly will!'

Once out of the surgery, out onto the bustling High Street, Belle's spirits soar, rinsed and freshened by the outburst, like damp greenery after a much needed shower. 'If I can't have a child, I'll get myself a little business. But not in this smoky furnace of a town; there's nothing left for me here.'

June 1943

'Where shall I hang the King, Mrs Morton?' shouts the waitress from her perch on a ladder, clutching portrait and hammer.

'Anywhere, Dorrie, as long as he's straight,' is Belle's distracted reply, as, swaddled in splattered dungarees and a turban, she sloshes on the last of the distemper in the newly altered dining room.

The senior waitress mutters under her breath – something about not being a builder's mate – as she sweeps up the dusty remains of the plaster work. The café had been closed for two weeks, so they could bash out the dividing wall from front to back, to let in light but more importantly, to squeeze extra tables into the dining room. Gone are the custard walls, dripping with treacle nicotine staining, the cocoa paintwork. No lunchtime shoppers with cheerful chatter and clink of teacups need hide the overall neglect of the place now. No wonder the three Greville sisters, former proprietors, are grateful for this quick turn-over of lease. They have no energy left to devote to such a busy establishment, now that they are preoccupied with a young evacuee from Birmingham, a little toe-rag by all accounts!

Belle tries to conceal her panic as she slaps the last of her savings across the walls, but Connie Spear is stomping sulkily with the broom. 'I mustn't lose my staff. I must stay calm.' She looks at each of them in turn.

Dorrie Goodman is a strange girl, but she's eager to please and her looks will pull in the uniform trade. Poor old Wyn Preece is stodgier, a simpler soul but a workhorse nevertheless. Connie Spear, the manageress, will need to be watched and wooed. Connie knows all the procedures with Food Office regulations and inspections, knows the best suppliers and what to order. Her bristling efficiency rubs against Belle's inexperience. Her obvious disapproval of the new regime is plain to see and hard to ignore. How long they will tolerate each other remains to be seen.

The café is in the heart of the bustling city centre of Lichfield, opposite the bus terminal, close to the market stalls and the Cathedral; a place where weary visitors can rest bunions and swollen legs, meet a friend and have a pee! Opening up the window onto the street will allow new customers to peer inside and read the daily menu, handwritten in a spidery copperplate by Connie Spear each morning.

Lichfield is certainly a crisscross of trunk roads, with plenty of 'comfort stations' for travellers to exchange petrol coupons, where troops pass hours at the cinemas and dance halls. For convoys of trucks, it is a convenient punctuation mark on the long supply treks, north or south.

The 'Cathedral Café' was only licensed for twenty covers or diners; hardly a viable number to make a profit and repay debts. If she can expand that to thirty placings, then they can receive extra rations and chits to cover the increase in turnover. Belle knows the theory. Now comes the real test: to compete with the multitude of cafés vying for a decent share of growing custom. Her secret plan to develop upstairs foundered on the rock of the upstairs tenant's refusal to budge from her billet. At the rear of the dining room is a door out into the courtyard and walled garden beyond. There are no funds left even to think about altering there. The rush to finish the alterations strains everyone's good-will. Madame Oblonsky, known affectionately by the girls as the upstairs Princess or 'Prin', complains incessantly about the noise and the mess. Connie moans about the indignity of it all. The two waitresses stand stock-still at the demolition.

'Hitler couldn't have dropped one better!' gasps Wyn Preece. 'We'll never get our old customers back!'

I hope not, Belle prays secretly. Please God! No more genteel ladies from the Cathedral Close in their straw bonnets and lace gloves, who perch overlong with a pot of tea, demanding constant refills of hot water, and who peck on tiny fancies from silver-plated cake stands, twittering all morning like starlings. New customers are what we need, with pounds in their pockets; passing trade with hungry bodies to refuel.

Sipping tea with dusty lips, they all stand back to admire their handiwork: the unboarded fireplace with shining Victorian tiled surround, the chimney freshly swept and waiting for a ration of wartime coal for cold days; the threadbare linen tablecloths, cut down into dainty place mats.

Dorrie has polished the dark oak tables into mirrors. With a posy of fresh flowers in season, the whole effect suggests a cosy parlour, a cheery welcome with flags and Mr Churchill on the walls, complementing the gaily printed curtaining backed by black-out linings. All this achieved on a threadbare budget and a visit to the auction mart on the Greenhill, where they discovered a bolt of printed linen cloth that the upstairs seamstress transformed into curtains, for the promise of some free hot dinners. Now there is only the final blitz on the kitchen grease and grime, more sloshings of whitewash and scrubbings of Vim and a shelf to put up for Belle's recipe books.

'What on earth does she want these old books for?' The manageress fingers a leather-backed tome with tissuey pages. 'Eliza Acton – who's she when she's at home?'

'A very famous cook, with lots of ideas for meatless pie recipes and delicious puddings,' Belle replies.

'What's wrong with our steak and kidney pud then?'

'Nothing Mrs Spear, but why not offer something different? If regulations say only one protein dish, then why not ring the changes?'

'Well,' offers Wyn, 'as long as it's not Lord Woolton's pie – that is disgusting. My mam had a go and it was like wallpaper paste!'

'We'll do better than that, girls – just you wait – stews and casseroles, spiked with herbs and spices. We can grow them on the top of the Anderson shelter.'

'You can't get stuff like that round here!'

'You can if you beg, borrow or steal cuttings. I brought herbs back from France years ago and grew pots on my window ledge. Herbs can hide a multitude of sins, revive an inferior cut of meat, tingle the tastebuds, I promise you.'

'When did you go to France, Miss?' Wyn questions.

'On my honeymoon, just before the war broke out.'

'How romantic,' sigh the two younger girls.

'My mam went to Blackpool with my dad,' Wyn chirrups.

'Maggie Preece's had a few more honeymoons since then,' whispers Connie, out of earshot.

'Did you go to Paris then?' Dorrie asks.

'We just passed through on our way south to the river Loire and the Châteaux.' She might as well have conjured names from the moon for all they knew.

'When will we be seeing Mr Morton?' pries Connie.

'I don't know.'

'In the forces you said?'

'Yes,' Belle mutters, 'hush–hush sort of job.'

'What did he do in Civvy Street then?' The questions come thick and fast; Belle bangs in the cuphooks.

'Not a reserved occupation, then?' Connie seizes the moment. Belle drops the hammer, an inch from Connie's big toe.

'Oh, sorry! So careless, my mind slipped.'

'I'll put the kettle on the hob,' Dorrie jumps in quickly.

'You've all done a good job. It looks ten times better, don't you think?'

'The Grevilles will be upset.'

'Why's that, Mrs Spear?'

'The Cathedral Café won't be the same.'

'How clever of you to bring it to our attention. A new owner, new premises and a new menu, why not a new name to celebrate?'

'What will you think of next, Mrs Morton?' Connie concedes.

'Something bright and cheerful, something optimistic!'

'The Cosy Café,' offers Wyn.

'The Copper Kettle – if we had one,' giggles young Dorrie.

'Come and see for yourself.' They troop out onto the street, where the sign writer is completing the bold lettering across the window boards: 'VICTORY CAFÉ.'

'Splendid,' shouts a woman, wobbling down the cobbles from the Close, on a black sit-up and beg bicycle, jam jars clinking in her basket. 'You have given the old place a new lease of life – we've been keeping an eye on all your alterations. Do you take bookings for lunch parties? I'm with the W.V.S. We like to support local enterprise when we have working lunch meetings. Hope we'll be your first customers?'

Belle stands in astonishment as a bright faced woman of her own age, in flat velour hat and red jersey, holds out a firm hand.

'Mrs Baverstock – Bindy Baverstock. Welcome to Lichfield, Mrs Morton. The Grevilles have told me all about you. I'm sure you will make a go of it. I think the new name is wizard, absolutely right for the times! Good luck!'

The cyclist wobbles off again, in the direction of the city centre, pedalled by a pair of legs as sturdy as tree trunks. The upstairs window opens and a familiar voice pours over them.

'Dear Gott! Is it all over now? All ze clankings and comings. When will poor refugee get peace from zis madhouse, you open ze 'Victory Café' I starving?'

Belle surveys her kingdom with growing excitement. 'Tomorrow is the day! So chop, chop, let's get cracking!'

Saturday Morning

Dorrie stared upwards to the buildings in the Market Square.
Nothing was changed, yet everything was changed. Only struc-
tures remained: salmon red bricks, roof lines, cobbles, the three
Cathedral spires; the Ladies of the Vale, guarding the heart of the
city.

Crowds jostled, muffled in bright colours, as once they jostled in
khaki and Airforce blue. Cars jammed the streets, where once the
convoys queued in ranks. Garish posters, gaudy blinds decorated
shop-fronts which once were taped and camouflaged in the dull
shades of blackout.

'Did I dream the war?' She searched out a familiar landmark
of windows across the street, counting them carefully, attic, first
floor bay, ground level. 'It's still there then.' She peered into the
darkness of the empty shop; bare floorboards scattered with paper.
'How can such an ordinary building have been the crucible of my
life?'

Dancing at the Victory Café

The reflection of a stooped, white-haired woman in a cream trench coat mocked back at this curiosity. Leaves scrunched under her feet as she sniffed the smell of autumn bonfires. Seasons never changed. It was November again; November was always her special month.

November 1943

Three dark faces peer through the window of the café on a wet afternoon in late November. It has been a dank dog of a day, rivulets of condensation trickling down the glass. Soon the blackout curtains will be pulled across, to close out the darkness from the 'Victory Café'.

The menu board is already tucked away under the stairs, there are a few visitors warming themselves over rabbit stew and bread and butter pudding (all in for 1s 6d), enjoying rib sticking stuff on a cold afternoon. At a corner table, the W.V.S. Committee hold an impromptu meeting over tea and scones, while whiffs of vegetable broth and baking waft across the tearoom. Mrs Morton, the renowned whizz with pastry, having ideas above her station as cook proprietor, tries to give the staff a baking lesson between customers.

Three curious faces peer in more closely, one face with eyes as black as prunes, the other more treacle coloured, sporting a pencil thin moustache and a cheeky grin. The tallest soldier, another khaki handsome face, has a cap set at a rakish angle defying gravity and rain drops, like sweat, across his brow.

'Dorrie! Close them curtains,' barks Connie Spear. 'We don't want no duskies in here.'

'Oh go on, Connie. It's pouring out there – they all look soaked through,' pleads Wyn Preece. 'Their money's as good as anyone else's!'

Dorrie Goodman pretends not to hear the bickering and beckons the men through the door. She likes coloured troops. At least they are polite to her in the street, not like the other Yanks from the local barracks, who wolf whistle on street corners as they eye her ankles. Always the same old tunes . . .

'Hi, Betty Grable, grab a wing! Howz about a souvenir, baby! You can roll my blanket any time!'

No, she is not impressed by their aftershave slickness or the razor-edged creases of their fancy pants. They are too big for their boots, too clean cut, a nuisance on two legs. The welcome given to them on their first arrival, a few months back, is now wearing thin. She no longer feels safe in her own city, unless Wyn and friends form a convoy. Even then it's two steps out of the café and up strikes the chorus:

'I'll have the redhead. Hi, Ginger Rogers!'

Wyn never seems to mind a whistle or two. Poor old Wyn has a mum, Maggie Preece, who runs her own Anglo American alliance, leaving Wyn to stay in each night babysitting her sister.

'Dorrie! What you go and do that for? We've been warned about them darkies . . . they are wild animals!' Connie mutters under her breath. 'All they want is fast women and you-know-what!'

Connie's virtue, in that case, is sure to remain intact. Dorrie smiles as she clears away the table for the soldiers. There is nothing fast about Connie. She is the sort uphol-stered against all contingencies, from her interlock utility drawers, army surplus 'blackouts' (special offer on Lichfield market), as sturdy as barrage balloons, to her corsets as blast proof as a Sherman tank. Connie does not believe in rush-ing anywhere. It is bad for your health, according to the Gospel of her weekly magazine. The upstairs door opens and out from the flat above, descends 'The Prin' for one of her frequent warm ups. She always likes to make an entrance.

'Come in, you poor boys . . . in for ze tea time. Meez Morton is a good woman – she no like to see strangers outside in ze cold. Look 'ow kind she is to me . . . by rights the flat upstairs should be 'ers since she take restaurant . . . but she good Christian woman, she take pity on all outcasts, on poor refugee like me . . . she no like you turn 'em away.

22

Beside I tell 'er, Connie, if you do . . .' The little woman
pokes a yellow stained finger into the cushions of Connie's
belly.

'And I'll tell her we were a pie short again last night,'
snaps Connie.

Madame Renate Oblonsky puckers her lips in defiance.
Her accent comes and goes like the tide. One minute she'll
be high and mighty, a Polish refugee from London, without
a penny to her name, reduced to sewing and mending to
earn her crusts; the next she can curse and swear at you like
a cockney fishwife and wolf down leftovers as if it were the
last supper. Leftovers are a thing of the past since the Greville
sisters sold the lease to Belle Morton. Leftovers used to be
Connie's perk. She believes the upstairs tenant is a sponger,
a thief in the night, but is saying nothing, for it is still early
days in the new regime. Connie escorts the soldiers to the
window seat with a grimace.

'What a sour puss,' whispers Wyn to her friend. 'My mam
says she'll turn milk. Always looking down her nose at us, as
if we were horse muck. Neighbours! You'd never think she
lived next door. They call her Mrs High and Mighty in our
street.' Dorrie nods in sympathy. She prefers 'The Prin'; a
tiny woman with her dancer's ankles, her hair swathed in
old silk scarves and shrivelled leathery smoker's face. 'The
Prin' is very old, at least fifty. Prin adds colour to the place.
You never know what she will say next. No one else calls

Dorrie 'darlink' or 'sweetie pie'. One minute she is all sugar, the next vinegar, crabby, whinging and tart.

'I'm so cold upstairs – pleez, just a cuppa offa cocoa, to warm ze bones. Av you a cigarette for a cold lady?' Bold as brass, she corners the three Americans and they doff their caps, duly rummaging in their greatcoats, handing her a new packet of Lucky Strikes.

'You darlinks. Thank you. It was not like this for me in ze old days, when I dance with Le Ballet Russe – when Diaghilev touched my cheek and smiled, "*Vous êtes ma petite fleur*" – such talent – so cruel to be injured, a destiny cut short . . . such artiste. Now I am ze nobody just delicate bones and such pain.'

Her voice trails away as she sweeps back up the stairs in a dramatic performance of the finale from 'Swan Lake'. Dorrie is not keen on all the smoking in the café. It makes her clothes stink. She knows it is sophisticated to inhale, to puff elegantly, as cool as Bette Davis and Joan Crawford, but the art of smoking hasn't reached their clientele yet.

The factory workers and Land Army girls cough and splutter as they gossip, the Brylcreem boys from the local R.A.F. station chain smoke as time for their training ends and they go off on night ops. You can tell from the state of the ash trays and nails bitten to the quick how many friends are missing or overdue. The local girls are always scrounging from the Yanks, who have the best ciggies, Lucky Strikes and Camels . . . not the awful smelly Turkish Pashas and cheap servicemen's brands. Sometimes 'The Prin' hovers at closing time and pokes about amongst the stubs for loose tobacco, to roll up her own with any dried leaves she can find. Wyn and her mum puff like steam engines. Maggie is never short these days, of tins of Spam, nylons or fancy stuff, thanks to Curtis Jackson, her latest benefactor.

Dorrie never smokes, nor would she dare. Father would never allow a woman to have such an ungodly habit. She obeys him, however, only because she knows it spoils a singing voice. Sometimes after work she arrives at singing practice and her throat feels so itchy and dry, she can barely reach the notes.

Singing is the one pleasure allowed to her. She sings in the Gospel Hall Choir. She sings in the zinc bath tub, to forget the thimbleful of tepid water and the plimsoll line. She hums on the pavement, croons as she peels potatoes in the café and knows all the hit parade favourites, Bing Crosby, Vera Lynn, Anne Shelton, all the popular musicals and operettas. Dorrie has begged for extra singing lessons but only gets piano theory and scales from Miss Fenwick, her old school music teacher, who is a regular in the Gospel Hall.

'You sing for the Lord!' Father decrees. 'Worldly singing is not for you.'

Belle Morton, the owner of the café, does not smoke either. She says it spoils the taste of her cooking. Belle has fancy ideas about her café. She is still a bit of a mystery to the staff but has certainly turned round the establishment into a modern café, with lots of good home cooking. Wyn says cooking at her home is something quick and easy, something greasy in a pan, with over-boiled vegetables, a push-past way of eating. Fast food is what Maggie dishes up: dinner on the run!

Maggie hasn't bothered to bake since Alun, her husband, went to war and is somewhere with Monty in the desert. Maggie has no need of a store cupboard now, having her own regular supplies. Not like Mrs Spear, who hoards like a squirrel, never misses a queue and haggles over lumps of gristle if she thinks there's a bargain on the counter.

The Cathedral Café always served plain food, simple and no fuss dishes, when Ruby, Onyx and Pearl Greville were in charge. Dorrie had been a Saturday girl then. Now, in the newly christened Victory Café, it is get them in, serve them quick and get them out. Keep them happy and coming back. The condiments are taken to the table, even the salt and sugar bowls have to be watched. They don't go so far as to chain up the spoons but the stuff vanishes if left five minutes unattended.

'Who says wartime food can't be daring? If they want Woolton Pie – let them go to the Civic Café, to British Restaurants, where you can fill up for a shilling, with solid food cooked in vats by the woolly hat brigade. No nonsense

fayre for evacuees and busy workers. Here we offer something more exciting. What is it, girls? Let's hear it?' trumpets
the proprietor proudly.

'Fancy food,' they chorus on cue.

'No, girls. We want colour, excitement. Food should be
an adventure, taste buds tantalised by explosions of flavour
. . . like they do, à la France!'

'Not any more they don't,' adds Connie. 'They 'ave to
eat frogs, snails, dogs, cats and worse!'

'That was in the siege of Paris, long ago. Now when I was
on my honeymoon.'

And out it would all come again, like a recitation, the
famous honeymoon trip to Paris, the journey down the
Loire, southwards; a journey changing her eating aspirations
for life: all those herbs with names like debutantes, the wine,
olives, pâté, truffles, smelly cheeses, simple peasant cooking,
soups and casseroles. Dorrie can mimic the speech, word for
word. The only information about the honeymoon is about
food, not Mr Morton, wherever he is or was.

Connie says that the woman who rents Mrs Morton three
of her rooms in Beacon Street has never once seen uniform
or boots in her cupboards. Her window sills are like jungles.
Apparently all sorts of queer smells waft from her kitchen.
The neighbours complain about the pong regularly and keep
an eye on their chickens. Her only friend is the bossy
woman, now sitting in the corner, wife of somebody in the

Cathedral Close, who is a chaplain overseas. Mrs Baverstock, the Bindy woman, takes up a lot of space on the table, calls the meeting to order and barks for more tea.

Dorrie smiles to herself as she observes her customers. People do give themselves away when they eat in public, especially their manners or lack of them, all the little revealing and revolting habits. She notes who makes a mess of the table, slurps their tea, takes their faces to the food in a rush to stuff it down quickly; who picks their nose and who never leaves a tip under the saucer. Belle is fair with tips, which are kept in a jar and then shared out equally. She never takes sides in squabbles. There is always time to take Dorrie aside, to show how to make crisp shortcrust, to cool it and roll it out decoratively. The cook is keen on presentation.

'The eye sees it first, Dorrie. Remember!'

'Slap it on, dish it out, what's the point? It all goes down the hatch,' sneers Connie.

Belle likes to fiddle.

Connie says, 'Fiddling is a waste of time'. She does not hold with fancifying good food. If the meat is tender then what does it matter if the potatoes are piled on and doused in gravy, or the Bisto pours too thick or too thin? Hungry folk only want their bellies fed and full, not food arranged on a plate, like a still life painting! Connie usually ignores Belle's instructions when she isn't around. She encourages the customers away from the more exotic recipes on the menu, with a snap of 'Off!' She then tells Belle, on her return, 'No takers for the jugged hare. I told you it's too much for our clientele.'

Bindy Baverstock never misses a trick though, spilling all the beans to her friend. How Wyn snivels in front of customers and could do with some Lifebuoy soap. How Dorrie behaved oddly around table 5 on Tuesday . . . Dorrie danced around table 5, all that afternoon, because she saw under the visitor's feet a mouse, stiff as a pork pie, victim of their latest poison campaign. She watched the couple kick it between their feet, waiting for closing time, to dart quickly with a dustpan and brush, shutting her eyes while she shovelled up the body. Bindy Baverstock usually compliments on a tidy appearance, on the neat black skirt and crisp white pinafore with pin-tucked bib and lace edging. Her lace cap strains, under precious Kirby grips, to contain a mass of copper curls, swathed reluctantly into the 'Victory Roll' hairstyle.

Dorrie is well aware of servicemen, who linger over their cups to watch her curve and bend across the table. 'Why not? I'm seventeen – my future is all before me. If I cheer them up on their dismal journey back to a bleak barracks then that's all part of the service. Some of the aircrews might be dead by next morning.' Hands on her bottom are not allowed. Once she has to spike a shin, to loosen a grip too familiar, and says loudly. 'Don't do that

SIR!' in a voice deep and resonant which, strangely, commands respect.

School is long since over; as are now the dreams of going to music college. She intends to volunteer early, to do war service outside the city. Her reverie is broken by the throaty yankee drawl from the boys by the window. They have ordered a mixture from the menu and proceed to pile the sweet and savoury dishes together onto their plates in a glorious gunge. This is common practice among some of the Americans. The rest of the customers fall silent as they watch them mix jam onto their ham salad. Dorrie feels oddly protective, aware they are the subject of scrutiny and sniggering.

'Is everything all right?' She steps forward.

'Yes, ma'am.' The oldest of the soldiers, whose hair greys at the temples, smiles and rises instinctively. 'This is sure a quaint place . . . we are mighty obliged for your lettin' us in.' The middle man is so tall, he has difficulty fitting his legs under the table and stretches out his limbs in the aisle. It is the third soldier who catches her eye and holds it just a little too long for comfort. She feels her cheeks flushing, as Belle staggers from the kitchen with a crate of pop bottles.

'Can we help you, ma'am?' The soldiers shoot up.

'No, thank you, I'm fine, but I can see another of your men standing outside by the window.'

Her words trail away as the café door bursts open and a military policeman, built like a tree trunk, storms into the room; a soldier in the familiar white helmet and gloves of a snowdrop. 'Get your asses out of here at once! Pardon me, ma'am, for the interruption, but these nigras ain't allowed in no joint like this.'

Belle steps forward to protest, 'There's no problem. They're just eating, like everyone else. No objections are there, girls?'

Dorrie stands alongside her. 'Not at all, Mrs Morton.'

The policeman looks her up and down and turns to the older woman. 'Ma'am – they don't eat with white folks, where I come from . . . regulations . . . not in a neat little outfit like this.'

'Well they do here. They are welcome any time.'

The policeman moves aside. 'Can I have a word with you all?' He ushers them towards the doorway. 'Sergeant Burgess McCoy at your service.'

'Yes, Sergeant?'

'Look. Hell! If they eats here, then the other guys will put your café out of bounds . . . boycott? Blackball, whatever you folks call it! You'll not get any regular GIs to sit in the same joint!'

'That's OK by me,' Belle smiles. 'I'm not sure I want the custom of that sort of soldier.'

Dorrie's jaw gapes at this boldness. No one contradicts the man in her house.

'I think you should reconsider, ma'am!' His voice is now steel-edged.

'I thought we were all supposed to be on the same side. I thought it was the Nazi fascists who were against Jews and coloureds. It seems I'm wrong about you lot! I prefer these gentlemen to stay, Sergeant!' Mrs Morton's blue eyes flash icily.

The red-faced sergeant wipes his face and suppresses his rage. 'You just made the wrong decision, ma'am. You just lost a mighty lot of customers, with real pay in their pockets.'

'So be it! I'll be the judge of that. Good day!' Belle replies.

The man turns, banging his helmet on the low beam of the door, and stands, his arms behind his back, waiting on the pavement. Dorrie can see the menacing tap of his restless boot on the flag-stone and the quick flick of his hand on his holster. The three men juggle together in conversation and rise.

'We're sorry, ma'am, for the trouble. We'll be movin' on.'

'No, don't rush. I mean it. We have no colour bar here.'

The men sit down again, after they have introduced themselves. The older soldier raises his cap.

'Chad Dixon, Supply Depot. This is my buddy, Abe Luther from Philadelphia, and this dude here, is Charlie Gordon, otherwise known as Lucky.'

Lucky clicks his heels in a mock German salute. 'We are sure pleased to meet all you kind ladies.' Smiling directly at one girl.

Dorrie can see the M.P. outside – watching. How dare he threaten the café? No fascist dictator could say who or who not they serve. There were enough flaming regulations in this war without scenes like this from a Yank. When the men eventually pay their bill, Belle escorts them to the door.

'I hope your stay in Lichfield is a warm one. It's an interesting place to look over, boys. Perhaps Dorrie will point you in the direction of the Cathedral just up the street.' Outside it is dark and wet.

'If you walk along the cobbles, you'll find the Cathedral Close.' Dorrie tries to ignore the bulk of the policeman, who has now collected a mate, both eyeing her with intense interest. 'On the other hand, if I show you down here' . . . she walks them over to the Market Square. 'All the best public bars can be found along the alleys,' she whispers. 'Go up, turn right down the alley. Then you can disappear!'

Chad bows again. 'You're some ladies. We'll be back to the Victory Café: warmest place in town.'

'Sure is.' Lucky Gordon grins and Dorrie feels a strange stirring sensation in the pit of her stomach.

They dart up the street and dip down the sidewalk, as she suggests, leaving the two M.P.s staring in fury. The waitress scuttles back indoors to report on the safe passage of the three soldiers to Belle in the kitchen. When she returns to the tearoom, the two M.P.s are sitting like ramrods, waiting for service. Connie moves forward but Sergeant McCoy, redfaced, bullnecked, waves her back.

'That one'll do!' He beckons Dorrie, who is puce with embarrassment. The W.V.S. meeting falls silent and observes. 'We'll have your apple pie and make it quick, little lady! And a large beer.'

'We've no licence, sir – tea?'

'Coffee will do, girl.'

She feels eyes searing into her back, as they light cigars and lean back arrogantly in their chairs.

'Cute little ass,' smirks the Sergeant, as he puffs rings of blue smoke into the air.

Dorrie struggles not to shake as she carries two pudding plates full of Belle's apple pie, crisp golden crusts, decorated with oak leaves, swimming in custard.

'What's this muck . . . where's the real cream, missy?'

'Cream's off.'

'So are we, honey,' sneers the Sergeant to his pal, the light ash now forming a tube. He takes the cigar carefully and stubs the butt straight into the middle of the untouched pie, smiling coldly, as he rises, his feral eyes narrowing, glinting in triumph at her embarrassment.

'Well, would you believe it!' gasps Connie. 'I told you not to let them darkies in. There'll be trouble.'

'Don't take it personally, Dorrie. It's not your fault.' Bindy Baverstock swoops like an avenging angel. 'I'll get onto his Colonel. No one treats us like that! Don't worry. He needs his backside tanning for that tantrum.' Under her felt squashed hat and her uniform, Bindy is ready for battle. 'Now you two are just the types I'm looking for. We've been asked to send a few girls round to cheer up the troops at Christmas – good girls of course, from reliable backgrounds – to do a bit of a concert party, entertain the coloured troops, tea and sympathy. These boys are simple souls, don't want them to get the wrong idea, do we? Nice sensible girls like you will do fine.'

Wyn is keen but Dorrie holds back. Her father and mother will not approve of singing and dancing, but if she can convince them she is assisting at a Christmas service, an opportunity to spread the gospel to strangers, then perhaps Father may waive his objections.

'You'll both come and do a turn. I've arranged for the dancing class to do some numbers. Cheer up, Dorcas, dear. It might not happen.' Mrs Baverstock, seeing her worried look, pats her arm.

Dorrie starts at her touch and smiles to herself. 'Oh, but it has, something wonderful has just begun!'

December 1943

'Mother?'

'Don't talk with your mouth full, Dorcas.'

The girl spits a stone into the pudding bowl. 'You know when Pastor Gillibrand goes on about the latter days, when the Lord will descend and meet His believers in mid air.' She stirs the custard with a swirl.

'Yes, Dorcas, spit it out.' Her mother pats thin lips with a napkin, repeating the text with eyes raised expectantly to the ceiling. ' "The trumpet shall sound and in a twinkling of an eye, we shall all be translated in mid air." '

'Well, what happens if I am in the Café serving hot soup and suddenly I'm translated, does the soup come with me?'

'What ever's brought this on, young lady? These are the Lord's concerns, not ours. You just get on with being saved and waiting your turn for the final solution. Read the Word, study it prayerfully. The answers are always at hand to the righteous. The Holy Spirit will sanctify our endeavours.'

'Yes, I know all that stuff, but what about the others, Wyn, "The Prin". They are my friends. Will they be left behind just because they don't go to our Gospel Hall?'

The mother sighs, shaking her head. 'The Bible says there are sheep and there are goats, the saved and the unsaved.'

'But it's so hard being a sheep when all your friends are goats, when they get all the fun, go to the pictures and the dancing, stay out after dark and wear make-up. It's not fair! Maggie Preece says you're only young once!'

'Short term pain for long term gain is what your father says. Your reward is not of this world. You should know that by now. We are a chosen people, put on the earth to pluck sinners from the burning, not indulge ourselves in worldly pleasures.'

Dorrie leans forward and smiles. 'So it's OK, then, if I go with Wyn and the Reverend Baverstock's wife to sing at the Barracks, in their Christmas Carol Concert, for the coloured soldiers?'

'OK! OK! Where do you pick up such slang? I don't know what your father will say. We don't hold much with Christmas – Christmas is for pagans and idolaters!'

'Yes, but it is a time when people think about baby Jesus and try to be good. Surely if we invite the soldiers to our services, that would be doing the Lord's work? We could hold profitable conversations. Get them all saved for Christmas,' Dorrie wheedles. 'It's lovely in the café, Mrs Morton has done it up, all tinsel and glitter, with a real Christmas tree for the orphan kiddies and Wyn's mum's asked me to tea on Boxing Day.'

'Your father does not like you mixing down the street with unbelievers, especially in a house where alcohol is imbibed and Yankee soldiers come and go.'

'Oh, please, Mother, we won't be doing much here. Christmas is just one long Sunday; nothing much to write to Sol about on his ship.'

'Your brother doesn't want a catalogue of the Godless goings on at the Preeces'. He's far too busy on convoy patrol to read gossip.'

'They're not Godless. Wyn's mum is very kind. Remember when Mrs Blake at Number 7 got word that her son was on his way home from a P.O.W. camp. Who was it that knocked up the street with a collecting box and got a street party going, got them extra coal and a joint of beef?'

'And look at the thanks she got for it! He was so exhausted, he couldn't eat a mouthful. All those good rations were wasted on him, poor soul.'

'But you always say it's the thought that counts. Love thy neighbour and so forth. Surely the Lord will whisk her up with us on Judgement Day?'

'Dorcas, I don't know where you get your notions from. Don't you hear anything in Bible class? If Father could hear this prattle at the tea table.'

'I wish you'd call me Dorrie. I hate Dorcas. It feels as stiff as whalebone corset digging in my ribs.'

'Dorrie is for the playground and you should have left that behind years ago, when you put your hair up.'

'That's another thing. Why can't I have it cut and styled?'

'Vanity, vanity, child, all you think of is outward appearances. Search your heart not your mirror.'

'So can I go with Wyn then? I'm sure I can get her to come and be saved at the Mission.'

'We'll pray about it.'

'When? I need to let Mrs Baverstock know soon.' Dorrie peers across the room, to the few Christmas cards dotted on the mantelpiece. There is no holly or ivy; no paper chains strung across the ceiling beams of their cottage. Photographs of Dorrie and Sol are the only frivolity on display in the parlour next door. Upstairs are three cold bedrooms in the eaves. One each for her parents and one for Dorrie. Having replicated themselves exactly, her mother once whispered, they have no need for further carnal activity, abstinence being a state of Grace. Carnal knowledge, much reported in the Old Testament, is still a mystery to Dorrie. Any reference to reproductive matters is never encouraged at home. Wyn, however, furnishes her with mind boggling details, too lurid to contemplate. No wonder there were only two offspring in the policeman's cottage!'

Dorrie crosses her fingers behind her back, closes her eyes and wishes for her Christmas campaign to succeed. Then she focuses them hard on her bowl. 'One for yes, two for no . . . three for yes,' she smiles. There are five prune stones. It's going to be all right!'

On the Saturday night of the concert at the Base, Dorrie and Wyn race home together from work in the blackout. 'I love getting changed at your house. It's all fish and chippy, always something happening. My house could be in a cemetery, for all the life it sees.'

'Don't be daft, Dorrie, who'd want to live in the middle of our madhouse?' Wyn flings open the kitchen door. A fog of blue smoke hangs like a pall over the room, where Marlene, Wyn's sister, huddles over the wireless with rag curlers sticking out of her head like unicorn horns. Maggie Preece stands, fag in mouth, ironing a blouse, her feet tapping to the band music, while Mutt, the mongrel, jumps up in delight at their entrance, trampling onto the open suitcase, full of dancing costumes.

'Get that damn dog out of here, our Wyn. What will Dorrie think of us. Hello, love. Your big night tonight. However did you manage to get their consent?' laughs Maggie Preece, shoving a mug of stewed tea in to her hand.

'Miracles do happen! Father cornered Mrs Baverstock in the street and she promised to be my chaperone. I could have died with shame when he collared her!' The two waitresses rush upstairs to transform themselves into chorus girls. Dorrie tries on a low-cut blouse from Maggie's wardrobe to go over her navy school skirt. 'I'm not appearing on stage in my Sunday Chapel frock. Look at it, fit for a funeral not a party!' The only indulgence on the corduroy is rickrack braid edging, in a mouldy green colour, above the hem. Tonight they Bisto legs carefully and Wyn draws a pencil seam up the back, trying not to smudge when she giggles . . . The blouse, tied in a knot at the front in the latest daring fashion, reveals a bare midriff. As she dabs on 'Evening in Paris' by Bourjois and pouts at her Coty red lips, Dorrie feels like a film starlet.

'Look! Eye shadow!' Wyn wipes her fingers on the dusty surfaces, on coal dusted rims around the furniture, then wipes her finger over their eyelids. Wyn knows all the tricks. Maggie pops up and dabs them both with panstick make-up, making a Cupid's Bow second to none on Dorrie's lips.

'I wish my mother was as glamorous as yours.' The girl sighs with envy at Maggie's painted nails.

'Your mother's home when you open the door. Mine is always behind the bar at the Goat's Head, fighting off drunken airmen. My dad would go mad if he knew what goes on there after closing time,' whispers Wyn.

The waitresses primp and preen in front of the cracked dressing-table mirror. The cream georgette blouse emphasises Dorrie's ample curves and she even brushes boot polish carefully onto her pale eyelashes, fringing them thickly, powdering them, to prevent smudges on her cheeks. Tonight Dorrie Goodman will perform in public for the first time. The butterflies flutter deep within her stomach. Soon they will dash across to the Market Square and wait for the 'liberty truck' from the Base to whisk them to the concert. Maggie gives them the 'once over' inspection.

'Why don't you let your hair down, Dorrie? It's too lovely to be in a bun. Here let me do it for you.' She brushes out the coils of red hair and rummages in a drawer for a bright red scarf. 'There, try this . . . red against red.' The vibrant scarf circles the luxuriant curls, the bow tugged down off centre.

'Knock 'em dead, kid.' She sighs. 'I wish I were seventeen, and all to go for! When I was your age, Wyn was on the way and that put an end to my gallivanting days for a while.' She winks.

The truck is late. Mollie Custer's Dainty Dots dancing troupe with suitcases full of costumes, stamp their feet and tap dance in the cold street. The littlest girls have headscarves over their ringlets. Their mothers, anxious to keep knees clean and clothes tidy, fuss over their offspring like clucking hens, with breath steaming into the darkness.

Marlene and Wyn will be as usual minus a mother. The concert is not at the main base where Curtis, her latest friend, would have given her a good welcome. Curtis is an M.P. and suggests she stays away from the coloured troops.

Bindy Baverstock and a group of W.V.S. volunteers have gone ahead by special car, to organise dressing rooms and finalise the arrangements. The girls let out a cheer when they see the two trucks, with dimmed hooded headlights focusing down, rattling into view. Their cheers are drowned by the roar of aircraft droning, thundering above, climbing upwards from the aerodrome. Dorrie counts the bombers in the dark. It is a habit of hers to count them away and count them back. She whispers her charm.

'Lucky moon, Oh lucky moon,
Bring the boys back safely, soon.'

The truck rattles so much that one of Mollie's pupils is sick over the side. The girls chatter with excitement, as they are saluted through the barrier at the main gate by the guardsmen on duty. The camp, camouflaged in darkness, is a toy fort of a barracks, surrounded by parade grounds and Nissen huts dotted on every space. The campus seems endless. Maggie informs them that there is a hospital and a jailhouse as well as huge hangars built for the Supplies Depot. It is rumoured that the prison there is guarded by a wild

Cherokee Indian, who shoots on sight if a man so much as puts a finger outside his cell, and soldiers are executed in the jailhouse courtyard. Dorrie and Wyn prefer not to think about such gruesome information. It dulls the glamour of the occasion. It is enough to know that Uncle Sam's Army is a law unto itself and they are entering foreign territory!

The concert party is helped down from the trucks and escorted by armed guards to a huge hangar. The little girls gasp in amazement at the spectacle before them. From the rafters hang festoons of balloons, garlands of glitzy decorations, baubles and streamers, American style; a fairyland of lights hidden behind sealed doors: another world away from their shabby Christmassy efforts at home. At the far end of the hangar stands a platform stage, swathed with gaudy satin drapery. Dorrie gulps at the vastness of the auditorium, her heart racing in anticipation of the coming performance. 'I can't breathe . . . I'll never sing in this, Wyn. Oh Gosh! Help!'

The dressing room is curtained off behind the stage. The mothers shake out the crumpled costumes, the cowgirl outfits fringed with lamp shade trimmings, the gypsy skirts made from blackouts, the boleros decorated with toffee paper spangles, the frilly ballet dresses made from old curtain netting. It all looks so tawdry in the harsh lights. How Dorrie envies the Dainty Dots as they step into their costumes for the first number. Just a bunch of schoolgirls who tap dance across the district on Saturday nights: rows of little Shirley Temples, with coiled ringlets, toothpaste smiles and bright rouged cheeks. Known locally as the 'Custard Tarts' they tap dance to routines in as regimented a rhythm as any soldier on parade.

The older girls, wearing pretty floral skirts and ballet shoes, wait nervously in the wings while the pianist checks the order of her music. From a chink in the curtain, Dorrie observes rows of soldiers shuffling in like a school assembly, bagging seats at the front on wooden benches, some sitting silently with arms folded. How different they look. So many dark faces. Dorrie's heart thuds.

'We're just another bunch of amateurs they have to endure. They must be sick of being entertained by well meaning do gooders. Whatever will they make of a bunch of schoolgirls?' The familiar doughty form of Bindy Baverstock strides down the aisle to the front of stage. An Officer introduces the entertainment and opens the proceedings with polite clapping. 'This is all a ghastly mistake! I shouldn't have come. It's going to be awful.' Tears fill Dorrie's eyes, and she swallows hard, her hands sweating. 'I can't get up there on my own . . . I'm not good enough!'

Then the dancing troops skip across the stage and sing.

'You are my sunshine, my only sunshine.
You make me happy, when skies are grey.'

They twirl and twinkle, tweak their curls, sway their hips as they have been drilled, moving with unison and precision; all except for one little slowcoach on the end who gets it all wrong – deliberately. The men laugh at their antics. She plays up to the audience and does it even more. Next comes the rootin', tootin' cowboy routine. The girls cartwheel, arch over in handstands and back flips, coil themselves like snakes and do the splits. After that number come tap dancers singing 'Ballin' the Jack', ballerinas floating across the stage as snow flakes. How the men cheer the 'big girl' items, whistling loudly. The show is all going down better than Dorrie expects.

The Dainty Dots are professionals, wooing their audience with cheerful noisy exuberance. The grand finale is the French can-can, which the older girls perform with a panache, shocking Dorrie rigid. To see Wyn doing such things in a frilly skirt and knickers; all those fleshy thighs on display! Not a blinker of embarrassment from any of them as they lift skirts and wiggle bottoms in the air. Thank goodness her mother is not here to chaperone her! The hangar is now in an uproar of hoots, stamping, cheers and thunderous applause. The 'Custard Tarts' are on form. The rest will be a bit of an anti-climax. Some members of the Operatic Society sing songs from their recent operatic production and the audience fidgets. All too soon comes her own turn to mount the steps onto the vast stage. The lights dim and she stands alone in the spotlight.

'It's Christmas. I know you are far from home, so I would like to sing for you all tonight, some of our ancient English Carols,' she whispers into the darkness. 'Away in a Manger,' she sings so deeply and huskily that there is a stilled silence. 'Lullay lullay, thou little tiny child.' She croons the second hymn and then, taking courage from the response, she smiles and begins, 'I'm dreaming of a white Christmas.' She beckons them to join in with her. The applause echoes round. Her turn is over.

The Yanks, however, have other ideas. On to the stage jump men carrying a drum kit, saxophones, guitars, placing themselves behind Dorrie. A microphone is plonked in front of her and adjusted to her height.

'Do you know "Bye Bye Blackbird"?' yells the trumpeter.

'Yes,' Dorrie whispers.

'Well then, little lady . . . let's do it! Sing some swing toons.'

The band strikes up. The drummer syncopates the beat. She sways her hips with the rhythm and sings her heart out, while the audience joins in. The deep throaty notes just pour out. All the pent-up restrictions are expelled with her first breath. Unrehearsed, pure instinctive musical flair enables her to take the cue from their nods and swing with the beat. 'I'll be seeing you, in all the old familiar places!' 'Jingle Bells', 'Paper Doll'. She belts them all out. In the darkness, Dorrie Goodman discovers the power of her voice, the power of her musical presence on stage, the dizzy pleasure of the footlights, the warmth of a receptive audience, this heady brew of intoxicating swing music. Performing is now so satisfying, she is reluctant to leave.

'You sure have one talented lady here.' A tall musician steps from the darkness in a tight zoot suit with gold braid and fancy trousers. Instantly she recognises Lucky Gordon. 'Let me introduce again "Little Miss Lichfield" singing with the Five Aces . . . Guys and Gals, Ladies and Gentlemen, give the little lady another hand!'

'More . . . more!' yell the girls in the wings.

'I never knew you could sing like that, our Dorrie, talk about hiding your light under a bushel,' smiles Wyn. 'Wait till I tell them all at the Vic . . . They'll never believe it.'

'No, no . . . don't please . . . I'm not supposed to sing like this.'

'Why ever not?' says the Bindy woman.

'It's just that Father says . . .'

'My dear, in dark times like this, we need every songbird we can to cheer us up. What's the harm in entertaining people? I must enter you in the Talent Competition. You ought to win outright! Your voice is so deep and so clear.'

Dancing at the Victory Café

Dorrie basks in the sunlight of their praise, hardly believing her daring on that stage. The benches are pushed back to clear a space in the centre of the hall, while the Five Aces continue to play on the stage. The concert troupe is ushered to the back of the hall, where a surprise supper has been laid out in the darkness, on long trestles. The tables groan with food unseen by the adults and children of the concert party for years. Bowls of salads and cut meats, beef, real ham, chicken, with baskets of soft white bread rolls, butter pats, cookies, chocolate fudge cake, brownies, candy bars, soda pop and a spicy dark drink, called 'Coca Cola' . . . ice cream cake, layers of light sponge, filled with proper ice cream and cream. The girls in costumes ravage the plates like starving beggars at a feast. Speechless mouths are stuffed with food, as they stagger with plates piled high as mountains, stomachs full to bursting, while that band performs jazz and swingtime routines.

Feet begin to tap to the rhythm and the girls shyly choose partners, to jive and jitterbug in the middle of the floor. The young mothers let themselves sway to the beat and the floor fills fast. Every woman, much in demand, dancing from partner to partner to partner. A gramophone is placed by a loudspeaker and the music comes faster and wilder. Dorrie hangs back, her feet tapping to the magic of the music, but its power is too hypnotic, she too drifts further out in a trance. How she wants to dance. It feels so good, so natural

. . . the face opposite her sways to the same beat, the smiling man beckons her, they move in a unison of motion. The rhythm seeps into her limbs, and they loosen in response, her scarf falls away, her skirt swirls and she loses herself in the jive . . . a hand smooth and firm catches her gently like a bird in the palm.

'You're good, little lady . . . real good.' It is Lucky Gordon. Her heart lurches for a second. 'Hi again, you were sensational on stage, what a voice. Can we hire you to sing with us?'

They dance on and as their eyes lock, a strange sensation pulsates through her limbs . . . their movements flow, each anticipating the other in a pattern of daring gyrations, welding together, each echoing, responding to the other. Oblivious of the rest on the dance floor who clap their approval. She has never danced in her life as she dances tonight. Lucky, a natural rhythmic dancer, guides her gradually and expertly to the edge of the floor.

'Thanks, Lucky . . . that was lovely! What a band.'

'You remembered my name?' he quizzes. 'What's yours again?'

'Dorcas . . . but I only answer to Dorrie. You enjoyed our show, then?'

'Sure did . . . a bit of sunshine in this dreary place. Sorry, ma'am . . . no offence, but England's a real cold place and I can't get used to all the rain and damp!'

'I thought you G.I.s had central heating?' says Dorrie.

'Sure thing but only the white boys gets barrack's warmth. We shovel boys gets tents and cold huts.'

'I'm sorry, I didn't know.'

'Oh a Jim Crow army ain't that bad. You gets used to it!'

'Jim Crow?'

'We's segregated. Don't mix . . . separate leave . . . different nights, different zones. Tuesday blacks, Wednesday whites. Jim Crow is what it's called.'

'I don't understand. That's not fair!'

'You saw what happened in your café.'

'It's not my café. I'm only working there 'til I get called up.'

'Well, what you saw ain't nothin' to what goes on! See Chad Dixon over there, a swell guy. Back home he's principal of a college, a varsity man. Well, honey, he's a welfare assistant now . . . Private First Class . . . education or nuttin'. We is all shovel boys, digging runways, loadin' trucks, driving supplies, store house boys . . . dig ditches like the chain gang! Not exactly what we's joined up for but there ain't no coloured combat troops. No sirree. We ain't fit enough to fight but do mule's work.'

Dorrie's eyes lower.

'Hey . . . none of this. It ain't your doin', little lady. We came here to help you folks out of a spot . . . and I am mighty glad I'm standing right here at this very moment.

You sure are a pretty sight for my eyes. I've never seen hair that colour, just like maple syrup in the lights; so beautiful.'

'What did you do before the war?' Dorrie smiles with interest.

'Nuttin' much . . . truck boy in Detroit, driving by day and jazz all night. I reckoned on gettin' an education when I's drafted. I reckon wrong. I got enough marks for training but somehow they ain't too keen to train up the black boy. We just here for the muscle but I'm learnin' fast!'

'So why do they call you Lucky?'

'I picked that up on the boat coming over. We zig zag across the Atlantic in one hell hole of a ship. For two weeks holed up in the bottom. I tell you, I dropped twenty pounds in that tub. Did we get sick! Some guys stayed on deck, watching the sea for "U" boats, too scared to go below. Weren't much to do but play cards or pray. You can get mighty holy when there's "U" boats prowling. So I play cards and keep winning. They call me Lucky ever since, Lucky Strike on the drums. And I'm sure glad I'm drumming tonight.'

Dorrie wavers, conscious that others were mixing among all the soldiers, reluctant to break the spell between them. 'I'll have to go, Lucky.'

'Wait, can I see you again? Will you sing with us?'

'I'm not sure . . . I don't think I'll be allowed.'

'Can I see you at the café?'

Dorrie nods, pulled by the bustle of the crowd back towards Wyn and the other visitors. His hand briefly brushes against her palm. They smile at each other shyly as she walks slowly towards the door.

'Bye, Lucky.'

'Bye, Honey Gold.'

'Come on, Dorrie Daydream . . . you're holding up the convoy!' Bindy Baverstock counts them out as a roll call.

Two girls are missing from the Dainty Dots. A brief shouting, shuffling out of corners and M.P.s storming through the troops to check out the men. The girls are half dragged from behind the curtained dressing room, pockets bulging with food, sheepishly grinning, as they chew their way through the ticking off.

'Just taking some home, Miss, for my mam and sisters.'

The M.P.s stand stiffly as the women are lifted on to the trucks. The soldiers file back to their quarters. Dorrie shivers at the thought of Chad, Abe and Lucky, making the best of it, in a tent on the windy Heath. She does not think much of Jim Crow.

It is past midnight when the trucks dump their tired cargo back in the Market Place. The Saturday night revellers stagger noisily along the streets. Constable Joby Goodman waits stern faced, as Dorrie jumps down. A siren wails in the distance.

'Where do you think you've been 'til this time of night, Dorcas?' he barks.

Mrs Baverstock steps in quickly. 'I'm sorry, there was a delay, Constable. The hospitality was so generous, we couldn't rush off.'

'Be that as it may, it is now the Sabbath, my girl.' He peers at his daughter more closely. 'What on God's earth have you daubed on your face . . . I'm surprised at you. Just get down the street and get that filth washed off your face before your mother sees it.'

Wyn and Marlene, clutching bags, follow silently behind the tall policeman in his cape. Dorrie, feeling the heat of indignation stinging her cheeks, strides ahead defiantly.

Marlene, thinking to ease the tension, pipes up loudly. 'She was really great, Mr Goodman . . . I loved it when you sang "White Christmas" and crooned with the swing band. They really loved her, didn't they, our Wyn?'

Wyn tugs at her sleeve but the damage is done.

'So you disobeyed me again, Dorcas, singing worldly songs, in front of American soldiers, making an exhibition of yourself before the ungodly!' He pushes her through the gate, while he escorts the two girls further down to their front door.

Alice Goodman sits in candlewick dressing gown, pale, gaunt, anxious, waiting to deliver her well-rehearsed admonition. 'Your father and I are burdened by your disobedience. We let you go out on trust and you repay us be dishonouring the Sabbath. You shame us before the unrighteous. Making a spectacle of yourself before coloured men!'

Dorrie shakes her head vigorously. 'Why can't you understand? They were kind, courteous and gentlemanly to us. It's Christmas, Mother. They must be just as homesick as Solomon, far from home, lonely and cold. What harm is there in bringing comfort?'

'Don't you talk to your mother in that tone. We know what's best for you. We have to preserve your spiritual inheritance, your virtue, your chastity. You belong to the Lord. You are not free to behave like others who know not His salvation. I think we should pray about this right now.' Her father moves closer. It is cold, freezing cold, kneeling on the linoleum with head bent, as his voice rises in supplication. 'Lord, deliver this frail sister from temptation and sin. Renew the spirit of humility within her. Teach her thy way of the cross. Forgive her weakness and immaturity. Bring her through suffering to everlasting salvation. For we know, the lips of the loose woman drip honey and her speech is smoother than oil, but in the end she is as bitter as wormwood.'

Dorrie bites her lips. The acid burns in her stomach, too much rich food rumbling her guts. The burp she cannot hold back . . . her father's stick comes crashing on her head, stinging all sensation from her. It will be a long and painful night.

★   ★   ★

Excitement bubbles in the Vic like a hot casserole. Mrs Morton flushes with pride as she pushes the weekly *Mercury* into Dorrie's hand.

'See anything there?'

Dorrie peers through the steam blankly.

The cook can't wait. 'Look – up there!' Pointing out a thin column of print;

'FROM OUR NEW CORRESPONDENT ON THE KITCHEN FRONT: BAKING BELLE. HANDY TIPS FOR CHRISTMAS TREATS'

'Baking Belle! Whose idea was that?' says the waitress.

'If we can have Potato Pete and Dr Carrot, why not Baking Belle? Don't you think it's a good idea to put the café on the map? Here, take it to show your friend upstairs and have a mince pie to celebrate – heavy on the apple and thin on the spice, I'm afraid.'

Dorrie gobbles it down, bursting to spill her own news, up the hall steps into Prin's flat, sneaking a toasted teacake on a plate, under her pinnie, out of Connie's radar eye. For all the Prin's fierce exterior, underneath she is as soft as marshmallow. Dorrie often lingers there at breaktimes, sharing her newly acquired baking efforts, hot from the oven, and sipping Russian tea in a glass. No one else drinks in such a fashion!

The café flat is only the upstairs of the old terrace house. The living room, cold, damp and musty, has the best view over the Market Square from its bay window; the floor is cluttered with paper patterns and material scraps. A paltry heat rises from a one bar electric heater. The tiny fireplace is full of butt ends. Above the ceiling are two attic bedrooms and a washroom. No wonder the Prin spends so much time amongst the clientele downstairs. Her blackouts are always flapping open, much to the fury of the Air Raid Warden, who threatens a fine.

'All my life in zat suitcase, Dorrie, when I come Lichfield. I get on a train, away from the bombings and blitzings. I stay on train till I think it is a safe place. I come in ze café, hungry and cold, I faint on floor and ze Greville sisters, such fine jewels, say I stay here . . . but zat Connie, she nasty piece of workings, she call me spy; no believe I poor refugee. I no trust her . . . but you are darlink child. I know you reach ze stars. I hear you sing like Choir in Heaven!'

'Oh, Prin . . . Can you keep a secret?' Dorrie dances up and down as she pours all the story of the Saturday night show and especially her meeting with the handsome Lucky Gordon.

'Be careful, silly girl! Men are vicked. You such a baby in zis things. I marry when I come first to ziz country. He is rotting bad lot. He vamoosh . . . poof . . . I no trust men after. All zes married women and soldiers, like Wyn's silly mother. Zis war is turning morals upsides the down. I no understand English woman – so stiff so starch but underneath, wild as rabbit.'

'Rabbits aren't wild, they're soft and cuddly,' Dorrie corrects.

'Zat so and they breed . . . too mucha sex is not goot for ze rations, *N'est ce pas*? Look Meez Morton she big woolly woman, she find a fella soon.'

'Will she?' quizzes the girl with interest.

'I see in tea cups,' is the firm reply.

'But what about me? How can I see Lucky again?'

'Bring him here then. We make tea for ze poor lonely boys at Christmas. We ask Meez Baverstocks, another woolly rabbit . . . they bring us rations and we have party, play cards, singa songs but you no tell zat fat cow, Connie. I make dress for Meez Baverstocks, I talk to her.'

'Bless you, Prin.' Dorrie plonks a kiss on the little woman's cheek.

'Why you keep callink me Prin?'

'Cos you are!' smiles the girl, counting the days to Christmas now with renewed enthusiasm.

'It's all fixed.' Those three words are the best present of all for Dorrie. Prin honoured her promise, somehow managing to inveigle invitations to Chad, Lucky and Abe Luther for a hospitality tea on Boxing Day, with special permission from the Colonel via Bindy's Committee. As Belle was visiting her friend in the Close, they were to use the café premises, on condition that Prin provided the fayre. For once, the moths fly out of Prin's leather purse, as she storms the queue outside the butcher's shop in Bore Street, ignoring Dorrie's blushes and the protesting customers in regal fashion, her five-foot frame hovering imperiously.

'Vot av yous got under the counter today?' she demands in a loud voice. The queue shoves and pushes but she refuses to budge. One look at her determination and the poor assistant rustles up some sausage and moves her on quickly to avoid a riot. Dorrie cowers with embarrassment. If ever a nick-name is deserved, Prin earns hers this afternoon!

Dorrie mumbles to her mother about her need to visit the sick and elderly on Boxing Day, as a Christian favour to her employer who would be away. Whether from guilt at Dorrie's recent treatment or in the Christmas spirit of goodwill, this elicits for once a generous response: some fruit, mincepies and slices of their Christmas cake.

The women set to work to transform the dingy room, hanging up paper chains and winter holly. Dorrie decorates the folding tables with care; there is bread and butter, cold cuts, even a few left-over crackers. The doorbell rings downstairs and her heart lurches.

'Happy Christmas, you guys!' The men doff their caps and troop upstairs. They enter the room like the Three Wise Men, bearing gifts in parcels containing a large ham joint, three bags of sugar and the biggest box of chocolates Prin has ever seen!

'Darlinks, you bad boys.'

The party is off to a good start. Lucky smiles shyly at Dorrie. They sit together stiffly, hardly able to bear the intensity of feeling between them.

'Hey, I brought my guitar so we can rehearse some toons. We want you to sing with our band when we give a concert.'

'I can't. I wish I could but perhaps you and me could enter the New Year Talent Show?'

'I don't think so, honey. It ain't easy to get a pass. That don't stop us singin' now.' He strikes up a chord. 'Give Madame a taste of your hit parade!'

They all join in. Abe strumming the beat on the table, Chad waving an imaginary baton. They feast on all the goodies and settle down to a game of cards. Abe tries to teach them Poker. Chad sits back warming his toes by the firelight, musing on his home town, Philadelphia, and his mother on her front porch.

'I'm agoin' to sit right down and write her a letter about your beautiful café and all the lovely ladies who is looking after her son, in such a swell fashion. I'm sure she'll be sending you a parcel from America, if I know my mammy.'

Dorrie dances to their music with each of the men in turn and Prin glides across the floor like Isadora Duncan with a silk scarf. All too soon the steeple clock outside strikes nine and Dorrie knows, reluctantly, it is time to leave or questions will be asked elsewhere. One beating was more than enough for her disobedience.

'We'll walk you home, honey. It's black out there.' The men rise.

'Just to the end of the street will do,' she replies.

They clear up the dishes, retiring downstairs to the kitchen, but Prin shoos them on their way. Dorrie and Lucky linger behind the others, who stroll ahead tactfully to ignore their whisperings.

'When can I take you out to the movies?'

'Not in Lichfield – father would kill me.'

'For seeing a black man?'

'For going in any Picture House. They are places of sin and temptation.'

'What about Tamworth, then . . . on my night out. We can hop on the bus past the barracks. What the eye don't see, it don't worry about, honey!'

'I'll do my best,' Dorrie promises.

Suddenly a jeep roars up to the pavement and out shoots the bull-faced Sergeant McCoy.

'Dixon! What the Hell is you doin', boy? This ain't your pass night.'

Chad stands to attention, saluting. 'All above board, sir. Letter in my pocket, sir, from the Hospitality Committee. Visiting the natives, sir.'

'Don't you be sassy with me, Private.'

'Escortin' the lady back home, Sergeant,' Lucky adds.

'Like Hell you is!' Burgess McCoy shines a torch into Dorrie's startled face, staring at her with foxy eyes.

'Oh ho! So it's you again, Ginger Rogers! Can't keep away from coon meat can you, babe? I got your number.' Dorrie flees down the street, near to tears. The jeep crawls along the kerb, stalking her brisk pace, making no effort to overtake until Dorrie reaches the Police Cottage gate. 'Hey, little lady, why you runnin' away, just when we've gotten acquainted. You sure is determined to get a bad name for yerself, datin' those boys.' The sergeant leans out of his window at his prey.

'No business of yours, sir, who I entertain.' She tries not to let him see her trembling.

'Oh but it is, little songbird, Mac McCoy is pretty choosy who he dates . . . I like your spunk and spitfire spirit. I likes a broad who's not afraid of a fighting match. I guess, we is just two redheads sparring for a showdown, anyday now.'

'If you think for one minute I would be seen with you . . .'

'Oh, girly, if you don't, well I'm a thinkin', yer policeman pa might just have to know, you is still croonin' the Devil's toons with nigger boys and he ain't goin' a be happy with that. No siree!'

'You wouldn't.'

'Believe me, babe, I would.' McCoy revs the engine and roars off into the night.

'Honey, is you okay?' A voice echoes from the street below. Dorrie scrapes the ice from her bedroom window in the eaves of the cottage, peering out onto the dark street and sees the torch flickering. It is late and the street deserted.

'Who's there?' She opens the casement gingerly.

'Honey, over here,' whispers the welcome voice of Lucky Gordon. 'Shall I climb up?'

'No. No. Hang on. I'm coming down.'

The night is starlit, clear, with a cruel frost silvering the rooftops, chilling bones deep into the marrow. Dorrie shines her own torch down the ancient pear tree, clinging to the wall, nailed by the frost onto the red bricks of the cottage wall. Please God the mass of tangled branches will bear her weight! The cruck-beamed cottage stands four square, set back from the street by a hedged front garden. It is a lop-sided, low building, yet the sight of the drop is enough to make her senses reel. A moonlit descent, icy and slippery, is the only choice. Father is still on duty. Mother is still at work in the kitchen under the stair well. Dorrie locks the bedroom door.

Muffled in a scarf and pixie hood tied under the chin, with Sol's old cable jumper over her pyjama bottoms, she edges herself out of the window backwards, praying, 'For what I am about to perform, may the Lord look upon this foolish handmaiden with mercy and a sure grip.' Slowly she feels out the branches with her plimsoll, as Lucky leaps over the gate to guide her into his arms.

'Lucky! You should be back in camp. Why did you wait? You'll get into trouble.' She snuggles for warmth into his greatcoat, sniffing the tang of cigars and good soap.

'Did that Sergeant bother you? I sees him following behind you. He ain't a guy to trust is McCoy. No one likes him.' They walk slowly into the darkness of the back alleyway. 'I sure as Hell didn't mean you to shin down the wall. You'll be frozen!' Lucky wraps his arms around her and gathers her into his chest. They kiss, gently at first, on the lips and she tastes the chewing gum sweetness of his breath. This is my first grown-up kiss, she smiles, seeing the fire in his coal black eyes. The beauty of him burning into her flesh like piercing arrows and the response is easy. They kiss then into a frenzy, drawing close, melding into one shape under the greatcoat, closer, closer into each other. Lucky breaks away suddenly.

'Hey, little lady, you sure know how to get a guy all steamed up!' They cling like limpets, laughing, each fingering the outline of the other's face, tracing the contours gently with reverence. 'Your skin is honey gold silk, so beautiful.'

'And yours is milk chocolate, smooth. I can see the moon shining in your eyes. I wish the world would stop right now and leave us alone here forever.' Dorrie shivers and snuggles closer.

'I can't believe this is happening.' Lucky shakes her playfully. 'It's like the movies, singin', dancin'. Before I sees you, I is a happy-go-lucky kinda guy ... easy come, easy go, kinda shy with the chicks but lucky with cards and beatin' out jazz. Now I's lucky in love too. Now I think of nuttin' only when I can see you. I keep droppin' ma tools, bangin' ma fingers, tripping over tyres all day long. Yer voice make me tremble when I hear it singin' in ma head. We just gotta do some shows together. Perhaps when this damn war is over, the Five Aces will be introducin' Dorcas Goodman, the Lady from Lichfield.'

'Oh, no, Lucky. I want a real stage name, a tinselly name to sing in, never Dorcas.'

'Dor ... cas.' He exaggerates. 'Cas ... Cassie. Now that's a swingin' sort of name ... Sassy Cassie. How about that?'

'Don't you dare, although Cassie's not bad. I'll have to think about it.'

'So when will my Cassie in the starlight sing with the band?'

'We're dreamin', Lucky, just dreaming. There's a war going on and you'll be moving on soon.'

'Dreams cost nuttin', honey. Why shouldn't we make plans?'

'Cos it won't happen. My ma and pa, they'll see to that and Uncle Sam, he'll see to that too.'

'We can sing at your church then.'

'Can you imagine them allowing the be-bop and the Lindy hop? Spirituals perhaps.'

'Ah yes, dem churches like de poor blackman's sad songs . . . "Ole Man River",' Lucky mocks, mimicking the minstrel style.

'It wouldn't work, would it?'

'No, Miss Bossman, we can wait till this show is over. It still don't stop us lovin' does it?'

'We'll find a way to meet. Come here, you big bear, and let me kiss you again. I like kissing you. I shall make it my New Year's resolution: to have a kiss from you . . . every day!'

Saturday Noon

The Tudor Café in Bore Street was just as packed with visitors and shoppers as it had been fifty years ago.

No one wants to see an old woman crying in her soup, thought Dorrie as she lunched alone, tucked into a corner out of sight; but the tears trickled, none the less. Why is young love so sure of itself? Nothing else matters. You think the world will stand still to salute you, wars will halt, to wait for love in a rush. Love in a time of war is a grab-it-while-you-can affair. How did we dare to make such schemes before battle, before night ops? We all did though.

Even Belle Morton. She had her fling and I was there in the Staffordshire bookshop in Dam Street, to record the event.

Nothing changes, everything changes; only smells remain to unlock doors into the past.

She paid her bill and sauntered around the market stalls, to the same bookshop. She sniffed again the damp must of old leather and remembered it all.

2
VICTORY PIE

<u>Menu</u>

Mock Oyster Soup

Shropshire Fidget Pie and Vegetables or Country Casserole with Herby Dumplings

Hedgerow Crumble and Custard or Batter Pudding (by courtesy of our laying hens)

February 1944

'Heads down and look busy!' whispers Wyn – the secret of staying employed in the quiet season.

The pavements are piled high with muddy slush. Everything looks so drab and dismal after all the Christmas fun. Mrs Morton has them all stripping cupboards, stock-taking, distempering, scrubbing the golden grease from the walls. Trust Dorrie to find herself groping down the back of the ovens for long-lost ladles and spoons, trying not to imagine what else might be lurking in the furry crevices to snap her fingers off. It is a relief to be called out front, to keep an eye on the dwindling winter trade, hugging the fireside seats. There are only the same weari-some jobs in the back, potatoes and vegetables to chop and peel, pastry preparation and slabs of bloody meat to hack and stew.

'Give us a chorus of "Bless This House", our Dorrie.'

Wyn attempts to raise their flagging spirits, but Connie Spear is in a foul mood.

'You get yourself behind that cooker and do a proper job this time, young lady. No larking about, you two. Her ladyship is on the warpath again with another of her schemes. Victory Pie Competitions indeed! Whoever heard such nonsense. As if we haven't enough jobs to do, without thinking of daft recipes to soft soap them judges from the Council . . . Competitions! Whatever next?'

'But Mrs Morton says it'll be good for business if we win. Besides, me and Dorrie think it will be fun to decorate the place in the spirit of Victory. Don't we?'

Dorrie nods.

'Oh yes . . . and who'll be doing all the work? Muggins of course . . . fetch me this and let's make that. Extra work is what it all boils down to, mark my words.'

'Don't be a spoilsport. It's boring doing the same old things,' braves Wyn defiantly.

'I can soon put a stop to that, Wynfred Preece. Just fetch a bucket of spuds and get them chipped up for the lunch rush and *you* . . . can take that look off your face, madam, too.'

'What look is that, Mrs Spear?' puffs Belle Morton, staggering up from the cellar steps with a brass box full of coal dross.

'Are the young fry giving you trouble! Chop, chop . . .

come on, Dorrie, you can come next door with me, to the bookshop. There's work to be done. Mrs Spear can manage without you for a minute or two. The Victory Pie is calling. Let's go and fling ourselves across the ice and find some new recipes to get our teeth into.'

To this clarion call, Connie Spear purses her lips like a pantomime dame but says nothing. Only the heaving of her ample bosom bears testament to disapproval.

The bookshop, for once, is not jam-packed with browsing servicemen, the sort whose jacket pockets bulge with these new paperback editions and who use the Vic as a reading room. Dorrie loves the heady brew of thousands of books, towering to the ceiling, in all of the poky rooms; all that knowledge fermenting away. The objects of Belle's desire are stacked high up on the shelves and they stumble through the dingy passages for step ladders, trying not to overturn the sand buckets and disturb the tranquillity. One look at the height gives the waitress instant vertigo, but her boss is hungry to see the whole of the cookery repertoire. Donning her reading glasses, she mounts the ladder eagerly.

'Must be hundreds of ideas in these old books,' she whispers, grabbing a book and fumbling in her bag for a notebook and pen. 'Look! Here . . . just what I need, spinach tart with apple puree, Herbie pie, Shropshire fidget pie, Walnut tart, Hedgerow crumble. We'll find something in this lot . . . Oops!' In the excitement of her discoveries, Belle topples into mid air, flailing backwards in surprise, onto a warm mattress. Underneath, a blue R.A.F. uniform cushions her fall. Dorrie leaps to their aid, stifling her amusement at the scene before her. The poor occupant of said outfit lies prostrate, with a bemused expression on his face, at this sudden descent upon his person.

'Good God! I'm so sorry.' Belle peers from her glasses at the startled young man. They both burst out laughing. 'I do apologise, I got carried away.'

'That's one way of putting it,' says the man, as he rises, brushing himself down. 'Neat landing, though.'

'You're not from round here, are you?' Dorrie chirrups.

'Down under, from Aussieland, Digby – Digger – Carstairs, at your service,' he replies, staring blindly towards the source of the voice above his head. Dorrie knows enough about air force uniforms to recognise the stripes of a Flight Lieutenant and the discreet ribbons of a D.S.O. and D.F.C. on his battledress.

'You have just been downed in one by the staff of the famous Victory Café, down the street.' Belle makes the introductions.

'Ah! The Vic! You do a good pot of tea, Missus!'

Belle quickly acknowledges the compliment. 'Yes and that's what you deserve after this assault, tea and cakes on the house, when you've finished browsing.'

'I'm easy . . . just passin' time.' He picks up her books.

'You from the Airbase?' says Dorrie.

'Yeah, bin there six months, drivin' me crazy, trying to teach the poor sods how to keep themselves up there.' He raises his eyes aloft.

His accent was familiar in the café. The Operational Training Centre, O.T.C. was always full of Aussie crewmen and trainers. Dorrie notices his tired grey eyes and the twitch of his cheek muscle as he speaks.

'Come on, sir, I think you need that cuppa now.' Belle pays for the books and the bookseller waves them out with relief.

As Digger Carstairs sits by the window, staring out onto the street, indifferent to the chatter inside, Dorrie feels a protective urge to shoo all the diners away, to sit down by his side and cheer him up. She is beaten to the task however, by Mrs Morton, who stuffs him with warm scones and rhubarb jam, her Yorkshire cheese tarts and broken-biscuit cake.

The youthful appearance of the airman on closer inspection reveals a rugged-faced man, compactly built, with sandy hair, square jaw, leathery skin wrinkled by years in sunlight; older than first impressions suggest. It's a tired face, taut and tight-lipped, flushed with anger. He stares past their eyes, as he patters off his credentials to the assembled staff, a home in Bathurst, New South Wales, navigational training in America and Canada, his dog Monty and his enforced grounding at the O.T.C. where he trains up new crews.

They all recognise the familiar war-weary expression, those listless repetitive movements, the flicking of ash, almost onto the tray, the way he circles the tin tray mindlessly around the table, the nails bitten to the quick, the nicotined fingers.

He is one of the many aircrews Dorrie observes tramping through the city, shadowy figures, muffled by fog and torchlight, wending their way down frosty lanes towards the firelight warmth of a cosy pub, a tinkle on the piano, a bit of a singsong, writing names in candle grease on the walls of the Goat's Head, drinking themselves under the tables if Maggie Preece is to be believed.

Often, at night, Dorrie hears their boozy hollow laughter outside her bedroom window, down in the street below, as crews wobble their way up hill from the city, back to the aerodrome and the next night's mission. Depression sits upon Digby Carstairs like a damp blanket, dousing his natural spirits. His own mother would hardly recognise the sagging features of his hang-dog looks. Inside Belle Morton, judging from her attentiveness, Dorrie observes a different interest. Digger is another of her challenges and she wastes no time taking the situation in hand.

'So what do you do when you're off duty?' she asks boldly.

He shrugs his shoulders. 'Bitsa this, bitsa that.'

'Look . . . I need a pair of heavy boots to help me dig over my new allotment, dig my veggy plot, if Digger'll dig,

I'll pay. You look as if you need a bit of fresh air in those lungs.'

Digger looks up at her for the first time, sees the brightness of her china blue eyes, the flush of her cheeks and saucy stare. He winks. 'Yer on, bewt! Anything to oblige a lady!'

Wyn looks at Dorrie, her mouth gaping widely. 'Did you see that?'

Being now a veteran in these matters, Dorrie replies, 'I think they've just clicked!'

The Victory Pie Competition grips the Vic like spring fever. Belle scours the allotments for vegetables in season for her experiments. The winter dampness lingers too long for good crops to sprout at her command. She enrols her new friend Digger in the search for spare cuttings and seeds. She churns out acres of pastry to find the blend which offers an unusual texture, colour and taste to catch a judge's eye and tongue. Connie Spear's patience is now as threadbare as the seating of her skirts.

On the afternoon when the former owners of the café drop in to sample the new tea cup loaf, Dorrie hovers by the window anxiously hoping to catch a glimpse of Lucky in the street. The three Greville sisters have for once collected their young evacuee, Sid Sperrin, from school all polished and scrubbed for the occasion; but he sits restless, banging his legs, eager to be off among the buses, in the wintry sunlight.

For once they take pity on his obvious boredom and allow him down from the table, to tear off his energy in the Market Square.

'He grows so fast,' they sigh. 'His legs are sprouting like rhubarb! We don't know how he finds the energy!'

'He's still Leader of the Salvage Club then?' Dorrie passes the time, her eye on the window.

'Not only his Salvage Club, but now he's into rabbit meat production and selling horse manure ... I don't know where he gets these schemes from! When I think what he was like when he first landed on our doorstep. He was Sad Ivy's son. You won't remember her, she was one of our girls, married late to a man Birmingham way, who was wounded in the First World War. Poor Bart, he died before Sidney was born. Then Ivy catches this bug and the poor child has no one. We couldn't turn him away. He's been a bit of a challenge!'

'That's putting it mildly, Onyx Greville. At your time of life to take on such a scally ... lively child,' Connie interrupts, shaking her head.

Dorrie looks forward to their weekly visit. Onyx, Pearl and Ruby, the 'Jewel sisters', as they are known locally, have kind hearts and old-fashioned manners; three Victorian ladies with bosoms like bolsters in the style of Queen Mary. She can still feel the prickle of the horsehair sofa behind her knees as she sat in their villa in Gaia Lane, while they interviewed her carefully for the post of Saturday girl waitress. Constable Goodman's reputation alone was all the reference they needed from her. However does Sid manage to keep his clumsy fingers from breaking all their delicate porcelain plates and ornaments? He is such a bundle of noise and speed. Dorrie guesses Sid runs rings around the old dears but they never seem to bother.

Connie whispers, 'Silly old biddies should have had a lodger from the Air Base. He's too big for his boots is Sidney. One of these days he'll cut himself, he's that sharp.'

As if sensing the comment, Pearl smiles. 'He's the best thing that ever happened to us, isn't he, girls? Such a mangy pup when he first came, so out of control, with sunken eyes like saucers and a head full of lice but he's brought a sparkle to our retirement. Given us a new interest in life.'

Dorrie nods in agreement; trust Sid to land himself such a loving billet.

Not all the evacuees were so lucky. Some families were trudging the streets searching for rooms, for cover, on wet days when landladies turfed them out into the cold. They were the ones who slumped in the café eking out a pot of tea and a bun. Sad-faced mothers with babies plugged into rubber dummies, while the snot runs down their noses, marking time, bedraggled, displaced and utterly ground down by the war. Even Connie hints that there are billets where the kids are expected to do all the chores, feed the pigs and chickens, muck out stables, clean grates like skivvies and to be fed on little other than bread and scrape. School dinners were often the only hot meal on the horizon.

Everyone is fed up with the drabness of life. Five years of rationing shortages, making do 'for the duration'. How Dorrie hates that phrase. Like a wet half closing day, her life stuck forever on amber traffic lights, 'for the duration'. Perhaps Mrs Morton is right to fix her hopes on something cheerful to raise the spirits. She peers out again into the street; no sign of Lucky and his gang.

Their romance blossoms in secret places, by stealth in the streets, carefully engineered soirées, band concerts, over cups of Camp coffee when notes are exchanged under the saucer. Chad, Abe and Lucky are regulars now and bring friends to spend their lavish pay on the best of the menu. The Prin occasionally invites them upstairs to play cards and smoke their cigarettes. Lucky and Dorrie swop passionate kisses in her kitchen.

'Dorcas, wake up, dear, be a love and fetch in Sidney, will you? He's going to get his only pair of decent trousers filthy. We'd never catch him.'

Once out into the Square, she glimpses the boy on a street corner, his mouth bulging with chewing gum, while a soldier fiddles in his pocket for candy bars. Trust Sid to be on the scrounge!

'Hey, missy.' A voice behind stops her stock still: the sleazy deep drawl of Sergeant Burgess McCoy. 'Hey, little madam. Howz about that date, babe? I'm still waitin' and ma patience don't last forever.'

The girl walks on, head in the air, tossing her curls, trying to ignore his banter, blushing fiercely at being caught off guard. 'Beat it, Sergeant, I'm not interested!'

His tone changes, the menace undisguised, 'I don't take no sass from Goody Two Shoes. You watch your step. I's a watchin' you, every step of the way.'

She feels his hand brush her skirt, smells the stink of his whisky breath, and leaps across the street towards the boy. Sid darts off at her approach. Dorrie, all guns blazing, roars at the lad like a cannon. 'Just you come back here, Sidney, or I'll tell them old dears how you skim down the trees at night. I'll tell on you. God help me, if I don't, Sid Sperrin.'

He turns his face sheepishly and smiles. 'You wouldn't?' In the thickest of city accents.

'Just try me!' She pretends to cuff his ear and leads him meekly back to the café, not daring to pause, in case McCoy is observing the scene.

Maggie Preece is soaking her swollen feet in a bowl of Rinso, listening to the Big Bands on the Home Service, when Dorrie calls in to collect 'the Mutt' for a long walk. The dog barks eagerly at her entrance.

'Time for a cuppa? Curt brought me ten pounds of sugar and real butter. Look, a tin of cookies! The girls are out at their dancing class, I'm all on my ownsome.'

'Go on then.' Dorrie looks at her watch as she shifts a mound of papers and unwashed plates to clear herself a place at the table.

'You keen on this Lucky fella then?'

'How do you know about . . .?'

'Well, Curtis says they don't hold with mixing with coloureds in the army. It starts bad feeling with the guys and big fights, you know, in some camps.'

'It's none of their business, is it? I think all this Jim Crow is terrible. I do really.'

'Don't you go mouthin' off about Jim Crow, especially when McCoy is on duty. He's a nasty piece of work, if ever I saw one. Just you mind it's none of our business. I'd hate you to get hurt. I'm hurting bad enough as it is!'

'Curt not a good bloke then?'

'Oh no . . . he's generous, kindly, what more could a woman want? But they'll be going soon enough. He says they're stockpiling stores, trucks. One of these mornings, we'll all wake up and they'll be gone, just like Alun, out of my life, as quick as he came.'

'Heard from Mr Preece?'

'Not for a month but mail's like that and then I'll get six letters at once.'

'Do you love Curt then?'

'Love? What's that about when it's at home? He's right enough but when you're stuck with a family, on a soldier's pay, with growing mouths to stuff, you just take your chance. He's lonely, I'm lonely. We've had a real good time. He's married, I'm married. Anyway, it's impossible to get yourself a Yankee marriage certificate. I'm not daft. It's just one of those flings, as the song says. That's what I'm trying to tell you, Dorrie. Don't go getting your hopes up.'

Dorrie gulps her tea. 'Who said anything about marriage? I'm going in the Land Army soon as I can. Anyway this is England 1944 not the Dark Ages.'

'Of course it is, love, but think on, some things never change. Love doesn't pay the rentman.'

'Maggie?'

'Yes, love?'

'What is it like . . . you know, loving a fella, properly. Does it show? Wyn says you can tell if a girl's gone all the way. It sort of shows.'

'Oh, Dorrie, you haven't gone and done it . . . that's how I got caught with Wyn. For God's sake, not with a darkie.'

'Maggie, don't say that! We love each other, honest. He is a gentleman and so kind. I love him, he's got right up my nostrils.'

'If he gets in your drawers, that's the time to worry. Do be careful. Has your mother . . . er, said anything?'

'Now can you imagine my mother telling me the facts of life? Wyn's told me what's what . . . don't worry. All they ever talk about is keeping clean and pure, like love in a cold bath. This feeling's not dirty. I want to get so close to him. I can't help how I feel, I never thought it would feel like this, melting together, sticky and warm.'

'You shouldn't be telling me this. I don't know what to advise. Just make sure he wears something, love, and don't let him spill anything on you. Believe me, you can get caught standing up or lying down. Please be careful. Loving fellas is a dangerous game. I should know.'

'I can take care of myself,' Dorrie snaps, putting the lead on the dog, bursting out into the dusk with furious energy. How dare the Army say her love for Lucky is wrong. The Yanks had strange laws, wrong laws. All this fuss about mixing socially. Glad enough to show off the jazz bands when they parade through the streets, wowing the crowds with their toe-tapping music. Put them up front when it suits them. No colour bar then! she mutters, crossing the Greenhill onto Darnford Lane, out into the dark fields with a flickering torch, watching the arch of a searchlight, feathering out in the distant sky. Why are we skulking in the shadows like criminals?

'Hey, babe . . . over here.' Lucky waits as usual under their tree.

★　　★　　★

Next morning she day-dreams, plonking the peelings into the pig-swill container, tripping over the fire bucket and sending sand across the kitchen floor.

'What's got into you?' Connie grumbles. 'Head in the clouds, feet in the shit.'

The morning is damp and depressing. Dorrie feels the fire of last night still smouldering in her belly; a restlessness to be alone pulling her out into the back garden.

'Hurry on spring and warm days. Hurry up world and sort yourself out. I'm seventeen and I want to get on with my life. I'm fed up with being kept on the back boiler . . . for the duration.'

The café, once a Georgian town house, still retains a sandstone brick wall, enclosing a pretty garden, cluttered with bunkers for storage and a small sunken Anderson shelter for a quick exit from the kitchen in an emergency. The corrugated roof arches over with soil, on which they grow fresh parsley, thyme and radishes in the summer. She sits on the wooden bench, hands cupped under her chin.

Nothing feels safe anymore. Her world is topsy turvy since Lucky Gordon danced into her life. Deceit is so complicated. Wyn is kindly but has no idea of the turmoil she experiences; lying to her parents, sneaking out of piano lessons, borrowing the Preece's dog. Any excuse to get away from home onto the streets. What she contemplates now, they say, is sinful and lustful, a punishable offence. This is no

Christian love sanctified by marriage vows, this primitive urge, rising straight from her groin. How can she begin to think of letting a man touch her privately, part her legs and connect in such a physical way. The power of loving between them is getting too strong to resist and now she is curious.

What will it be like, that first time? Once can do no harm . . . just to prove how much she loves him. It must be love; this thunderous cloud crashing over my head. Is it visible, this passion? Does it swirl out of me like a halo? Why else do I feel so different, so special, so alive? Now is our time. It might never happen again. Whatever the war might bring, sudden partings, perhaps death. Once will be safe. Dorrie feels her limbs trembling at the thought of the disobedient act of love. Restraints weaken, loosening like worn elastic. Who knows when Lucky will be posted overseas? I must send him away loved, remembered, satisfied. Lucky is my love, the door to life.

'Dorrie Goodman, get back inside and stop all this day-dreaming. There's a war on and thirty hungry customers to be served.' Belle Morton's shrill call to arms douses her stirrings like a splash of cold water. 'See if the chickens have done their duty yet!'

She dawdles to the coop in the corner of the wall and the chickens scatter in protest as she ferrets gingerly in the nesting boxes. There are three eggs again. The creatures are responding to the stronger daylight. Soon a dozen speckled eggs will boost the dried egg powder to make the fluffiest scrambled eggs or sponge batter. Spring is on its way!

'Now, girls,' says Belle after the lunchtime rush, when they collapse for a quick sandwich and a breather, before the afternoon tea brigade arrive, 'I want you to know, I'm giving this Victory Pie competition serious thought. In fact I've made one or two experiments.'

Three waitresses nod, as they glance over Belle's burgeoning skirt. Belle, with her broad hips and curvaceous figure, is the epitome of a cook who tastes her fayre. Her arms are as plump but firm as her thighs. Her fair hair, gathered on the top of her head, is in the latest pompadour style, piled high in neat sausage rolls, a style which heightens the curve of her arching brow, high cheekbones and sapphire eyes. Not for Belle the usual tight curls anchored by a battery of hair pins, the pencilled brow or pillar box lips. In the kitchen Belle is a firm believer in all the principles of hygiene, however unglamorous, and joins the others wearing their tight skivvy mob caps. 'I don't want any of my customers to have to pick hairs out of their soup or snot from their sandwiches, as I did once in a certain rival establishment nearby.'

Belle loves her food and the evidence spreads around her belly, from too many teacakes dripping with butter, to jam omelettes and batter puddings. Today she is in an abstemious mood. 'What we need is a philosophy!'

The women wait, curious as to the explanation. Connie folds her arms in defiance. 'Here we go again, more work!' she mutters.

'When is the darkest hour?' Belle begins.

'Before the dawn,' pipes Dorrie.

Connie gives one of her best withering glances. 'Little show off.'

'That's right. Our victory can't be far away . . . six months, a year at most. What we need is to cheer the darkest hour with something filling, but different. The memory of a good meal lingers on long after the goodness has been absorbed by the body. It lingers like a sweet melody, seducing the taste buds, mouth salivating . . . tangy, spicy, succulent juices. When victory finally comes, it won't only be ours alone, will it? We owe it in some part to all our allies, the free French, Poles, Americans, Colonies, Empire. So why not create a menu to reflect all this combined effort. All our allies in a glorious mixture of ingredients. What do you think?'

'How the devil can you get stuff from India or Australia or Poland?' Connie sniggers.

'We've had enough of drab food, of stodgy utility recipes. Let's go for something exotic . . . spices from the Caribbean, pineapple chunks, melons, peppers, bananas, tamarind, fenugreek, cardamon. Oh, for the taste of something different!'

'All we've got is ham, Spam and pickles,' reminds Wyn.

'I think it's time to unlock our secret stores, the hidden treasure trove of spices, the brandied fruits, bottled pears, the preserves kept back for just this occasion. Their time has come. Let's throw caution to the wind. Stir up, oh Lord, thy servants with thy spirit.'

'She's been at the damson gin,' whispers Connie, leaning forward for a whiff of breath.

'No, no. This Victory Pie must be a hymn to the future triumph, a paean of praise for all the effort put into our survival. Girls! We are going to win or burst in the attempt!'

No one has seen Belle so animated, so out of her usual workaday self, so crazy, so intense.

'If it isn't gin, then it must be love,' Connie sniffs. 'It's that daft Digger from down under. The dreamy Aussie with his head in a book and the silly grin. He's turned her head and addled her brains!'

The parcel sits like an unexploded bomb on the table, while the staff circle around, examining the foreign stamps, the battered brown paper and the label, with reverence: Madame Renee Oblonsky-White, C/o 'Victory Café'.

'It's a food parcel from America,' says Wyn in hushed voice as she fingers the wax seals. 'One of them bundles for Britain, from our allies and for Prin!'

'Who's this Renee White then? I told you she was a confidence trickster,' adds Connie.

'She told us she married, remember?' replies Dorrie.

'She's no refugee then, is she?'

'Yes I am.' Prin rushes down the stairs. 'From bombings and blitzings, shut your face.' The tiny woman prods the parcel in disbelief, trying to unknot the string with nicotined fingers. Excitement mounts as she tears at the wrappings, like a terrier down a rabbit hole. Inside are small tins of Canadian salmon, American ham roll, wrapped around stockings and socks, stuffed with small packets of spices, labelled for the cook. There are scented soaps and a card of elastic. Buried in the heart of the parcel is a squashed box of pink marshmallows! 'I never havze birthday like theez!! Who give me such kind present?'

Dorrie examines the labels. 'It's Dixon, Philadelphia, from Chad's mother. She's sending us a thank you, from Chad.' She picks out a small note and a crumpled photograph of his family on the porch of their house, tucked in the packaging.

'Open the sweets then,' urges Connie, licking her lips.

'No, I take these up ze stairs.' Prin hugs the parcel tightly into her bodice.

'You mean old crone, not giving your friends a taste.'

'Leave her. It's her parcel not yours. She's the one who gives them her tea. You were for not letting them come in the café at all, Mrs Spear,' shouts Dorrie and Wyn nods her support.

'Look at all them spices . . . won't Mrs Morton get a surprise. Ginger powder, cinnamon sticks and allspice. Look, real black peppercorns. Just what she needs for her Victory Pie.'

'I think it's a waste of good food and effort,' snorts the Manageress.

'You would,' giggle Wyn and Dorrie to themselves, as they polish the table tops into waxy mirrors.

'I hear your Sol's on his way home from sea,' says Wyn, making no secret of her interest in the photo in Dorrie's purse.

'Tonight if they dock on time. I can't wait to see him. It's been two years.'

'I bet he's changed a lot.'

'We've all had to change, haven't we?' Dorrie answers, making faces at her reflection on the glossy table.

'Your dad never changes, does he?'

'That's because he's preserved in religion,' laughs Dorrie. 'Like pickled onions sealed in a jar!'

'You do say some queer things, Dorrie Goodman. How's it going with lover boy?'

'Okay.'

'Only Okay? Have you done anything you shouldn't yet?'

'Mind your own business, Wynfred Preece,' blushes Dorrie.

'You will tell me what it's like, if you do. I'm dying to know.'

'My lips are sealed.'

'Are you preserved in religion, as well?' Wyn retorts.

'You must be joking. Two jars of pickled preserves in our house is quite sufficient, thank you.'

Everyone is in a good mood for once, now that Sol is on his way home for a week of precious leave. Mother hums choruses as she sifts the grey gritty National flour through her fingers: 'Will your anchor hold in the storms of life.'

Tonight the parlour fire blazes in honour of his return. The table is festooned with the whitest starched cloth, with embroidered corners covered in gaudy pink and purple hollyhocks. The last of the pre-war salmon, hoarded so carefully for just such an occasion, has been opened, mashed with vinegar and margarine, to eke out the sandwiches and cold meat platter alongside Dorrie's favourite summer pudding.

Solomon has served on escort vessels in the Atlantic for three years; a dangerous mission. Torpedoed once, but saved by swimming to some wreckage and picked up promptly. He had been working deep in the engine room but had been sent up on deck, at the far end from the explosion, a lucky escape, which Alice Goodman puts down to all her praying. Now all her kneeling has another reward.

Dorrie tweaks the curtains anxiously. 'Can I go and meet the train?'

'Your Father is quite capable of doing that. You keep at your piano practice. Give Sol some idea of your progress. You know there's an exam coming up. Miss Fenwick says you're getting a bit slapdash these days. She keeps asking me if I am recovered and said something about you having to finish early on Tuesdays. That's news to me, I told her. The Goodmans are all blessed with the best of health. A tranquil mind gives life to the flesh, only "Passion makes the bones rot", I reminded her.'

Dorrie feels the heat of her guilt rising in her cheeks but bluffs away the accusation. 'Oh, Miss Fenwick's always getting me muddled with Vera Hill. Her father's very sick.' No one suspects that Lucky sneaks under the camp fence and meets her each Tuesday beneath the railway arch, walking her as far as is safe. The lies burn her throat. 'I hear Pastor Gillibrand has invited the Gospelairs from the Base to sing on Sunday night. Sol will enjoy it if I sing alongside them in the choir. I can't wait to see his face . . . do you think I've grown?'

'Don't fuss so about your appearance. Handsome is as handsome does, Dorcas. Go on and do your practice.'

For once, her restless fingers find solace in tearing up and down the keyboard. Sol, her big brother, is her only ally in this dreary household. He will cheer her up with tall tales. She will be allowed out with him to chaperon her.

Wyn will make some excuse to call in. Wyn fancies the tall lanky seaman, says he looks just like Robert Donat in the 'Thirty Nine Steps'. It is very late when she hears the door opening and the noise of voices in the hallway. The trains are a law unto themselves and Sol's arrival is several hours later than expected. She waits for her parents to see him alone for a few seconds, hanging back to let them savour his company. Sol will soon seek her out. The door opens, she flings her arms blindly around him.

'Oh Sol . . . Thank God. It's so lovely to have you home.' She buries herself in his uniform, sniffing the stale tobacco smoke, the sweaty aroma of a tired seafarer.

'Well, sis, let me see, quite the young lady.'

She twirls around for him to admire the view. 'How was your journey?'

'Terrible . . . the train time forgot. We were stuck in a siding for an hour, cramped up like sardines while an air raid nearly severed the track. We all just had to sit it out, poor Yanks from the Heath, stuck there so long, ruined their evening too. Hope you don't mind, this poor guy had been on leave in London, missed all his connections, so I've brought him home for the night or at least 'til he can pick up a liberty truck back to Base.'

'Oh, Sol, I wanted to see you by yourself. Trust you to pick up some stranger, typical!'

'Not exactly . . . he says he knows you from the café. Nice friendly guy, just your sort. We thought you'd like a little excitement. He's talking round father. Here, see, let me introduce you to . . .'

Dorrie nearly faints at the sight of the smiling man filling the door frame.

'H'ya, Miss Goodman. I told yer brother, we're old sparring partners.' There stands Burgess McCoy, grinning triumphantly, stalking through her cottage like a smiling tiger. Dorrie steps back weakly.

'Hello, Mr McCoy,' she replies coldly. 'My brother seems to think he owes you hospitality. I would have thought the buses are still running to the Heath. It's only a three mile walk.'

'See what I mean? Such a spark in your sister. When I finds out Solly boy is your big brother . . . why, I told him how obliging you were – what a little songbird.' The coded message is clear. You treat me well or I spill the beans. They sit at the table stiffly, while Father says his favourite Grace for visitors. An aching disappointment seeps through her limbs. This was to be Sol's special night; not shared with a bully like McCoy.

'Dorrie eat up, you're wasting good food,' says Mother.

'I'm not very hungry.' Dorrie sulks, her head bowed so as not to catch the Yank's piercing eyes.

'It seems my daughter has lost her manners. She's still a silly girl at times. Sergeant Burgess is from Atlanta, Georgia. He attends the Southern Baptist Church and is in fellowship with all Bible based churches.'

'Is that a church extended to all believers, Mr McCoy?' Dorrie cannot resist the challenge.

'It sure is. We believe in salvation by the blood of the Lamb – the wages of sin is death and the damned are redeemed through the blood of Jesus alone. There is no salvation any other way.'

'Alleluia!' Joby Goodman echoes. 'Praise the Lord! It is our honour to share our table with a companion of the Lord. We hope you'll visit our service on Sunday at the Gospel Hall. Come and tell the folks round here all about Christian Witness in Atlanta.'

'In Christ there's no slave or free, male or female, is that so Mr McCoy?'

'Why yes, so the Bible says.'

'That's hardly what I hear about the way they treat slaves in the south!'

'There ain't no slaves, missy.' His voice hardens. 'The nigras worship in their own churches as they wish.'

'Please forgive my daughter. She has forgotten herself. Dorcas, apologise to the Sergeant, he is a guest in our house.'

'Your daughter is entitled to her opinion. She can't understand our ways. I would be honoured to instruct her further, so that she can look kindly on this simple soul. She sure has a temper with that hair. I think we can come to some understanding, little lady, can't we?' The threat now barely concealed.

She feels his knee push hard onto her thigh under the table and shoots up from her seat. 'I don't feel well. Please excuse me.' She rushes upstairs, flinging herself onto the bed in tears.

Later comes a tap tap, as Sol peers anxiously round the door. 'Dorrie, what's up? It's not like you to be so rude!'

'Oh Sol, Burgess McCoy's an awful man. He's been watching me, you know how some Yanks can pester a girl. I don't like him, Sol. He makes my skin crawl with ants. Get rid of him, please, I'm not coming down again, no matter how hard Father belts me.'

'Is he at it again, love? You'll get no beating while I'm in the house, I promise. I'm sorry, kiddo. What's this guy done to you, to upset you so? He was so chummy on the train.'

'He only used you to get in here, to butter up Father with his phoney preacher stuff. I don't trust him. He treats the coloured soldiers badly . . . Curtis Jackson, that's Maggie Preece's friend from the Base, doesn't trust him either. He warned me against crossing him.'

'These bleedin' Yanks don't own the place,' Sol snaps. 'Don't worry, sis, I'll sort is out, sorry I started all this, sorry, love.'

'You weren't to know. He can be very cunning. Just get rid of him. Don't let him stay in the house tonight.'

'Don't you worry, I'll take him out for a drink, out of harm's way.'

No one knows how or where the battle of Lichfield begins that weekend but it spreads street by street, skirmish by skirmish, throughout the public bars. From the Turk's Head to the Scales . . . through to the Earl of Lichfield and into the Goat's Head and the Talbot, the Dirty Duck, the Queen's Arms. Flames, fanned by rumours that a local girl has been insulted, raped, forced at knife point, murdered by one, two, three gangs of Yankee thugs and now lies at death's door in the Cottage Hospital.

A bunch of Polish pilots, grounded in the city, thick fog on the airfield having cancelled all flights, whoop and wail like banshees, crashing chairs, bottles – in a saloon brawl fit to be dished up in a western. Suddenly the streets are cleared of any Yankee uniforms by Military Police.

The police are baffled. Not a single complaint has been received that night. Nothing occurs to warrant such an explosion of indignation. The arrested are slung in the lock-ups in the Guild Hall and allowed out later, with a caution. From her vantage point in the attic window, the Prin sees all: how Yankee snowdrops barricade themselves like a wagon train under attack from Indian hordes; how Solomon

Goodman slugs it out with that nasty sandy-haired sergeant, who holds his groin from the blows. 'You call my sister a whore once more and I'll see you in Hell, you hypocrite.'

'Zat big brother of you, he shout and kick him in balls. Such excitement I no see, since the crowds storm ballet to see Nijinsky wizout ze tickets.'

Next morning the publicans mop the blood, repair the damage, sweep up the smashed glass and count their takings. Fighting is thirsty work and the barrels of weak wartime beer are well and truly drained to the dregs. Dorrie keeps out of sight, dodging her parents' questions about Sol's black eye, refusing to explain the sudden departure of Sergeant McCoy back to barracks.

Lucky and Co were confined to barracks during the riots but jungle drums beat wildly about the affray. Dorrie edits her account carefully but the young soldier warns, 'One night McCoy'll find himself outnumbered in a dark alley.'

'He's not worth it, Lucky. Please forget it. It'll only draw attention to us. He'll get you a posting to another camp, if he can. I couldn't bear that.'

'But it ain't fair, Dorrie.'

'None of this is fair . . . all this hiding. My father would kill me if he knew I was dating a soldier. He's got strange ideas. He'd follow me, and spoil it all.'

'McCoy is real mean. He's got some deals going on. Who hasn't on this goddam base? Curt Jackson's okay, fair enough, but one M.P. watching the other M.P. What a way to win a war.'

'The day of judgement is upon us!' yells Belle to her staff. 'We've got a date for the Victory Pie Competition. Here, soak these beans. I'm going to turn them into a Bean Bake with belly pork, mustard and molasses and some herbs, if I can find any fresh ones.'

The red, white and blue theme causes them all a problem, as they piece together old bunting and flags to make a patriotic display. Marlene Preece's paint box is stripped bare of all the carmine and Prussian blue to make flag labels, illustrating national dishes. No detail is too much effort. Judging will soon commence and the awards will be announced at the next National Savings Parade.

'We're not doing tomato soup. It's too predictable. I've still got some beetroot stored in sand. We are going to have Bortsch.'

'What's that then?' demanded Connie.

'Beetroot soup.'

'More foreign muck,' she sighs. 'What's wrong with calling it what it is, beetroot soup?'

'Because it sounds better and is more complicated. We want to link it with our allies on the eastern front, the Poles, the Russians. I thought about "Stalin's Surprise" but that's going over the top a bit. Our Victory Pie has to meet all the criteria, a protein main dish – beans in bacon or pork, with pickled red cabbage and carrot and turnip mashed together . . . cheerful don't you think? It's the blue pudding which I can't sort yet. Any ideas?'

'Blackberries or plums,' Wyn suggests. 'Or bilberries?'

'Too early in the season. I made last year's into jam, but we still might get some bottled from the W.I. and add apples to eke it out a bit, a bilberry fool perhaps?'

'She's a fool if she thinks anyone'll eat that.'

'Shush, Mrs Spear, I think it's original, a red, white and blue meal.' Dorrie is relieved to get away from the tensions at home now Sol has departed. Father, who senses her back-sliding, has enlisted Pastor Gillibrand to involve her in more activities at the Gospel Hall. They plan some Evangelical 'Outreach' to all the service folk, expecting her to sing at each service, to raise the emotional temperature in the Gospel Hall as she sings, 'Just as I am, without one plea. But that Thy blood was shed for me'. Singing, to seduce the wavering sinners out front, to join the Pastor at the pulpit rail and get themselves saved.

'Wake up, Dorrie Daydream. We can gain extra points by extending the theme to other items, cakes, fancies, even decor.' Belle struggles to recapture their waning enthusiasm.

Lichfield bustles with troops on the move and there is little time even to clear the tables before the next onslaught of starving customers gobble up the menu. Wyn says the whole world is cranking up a gear, ready for the last hard uphill slog home, to peace.

'Curtis told my mam that they're emptying all the jails back home and shipping them over here. Gangsters arrive still with handcuffs on them. It's getting near to boiling point up on the Heath, not an inch of turf left. They are ready for the Big Push, cancelling all leave, just in case. Isn't it exciting?'

Dorrie shrugs her shoulders nonchalantly; inside she feels like screaming. Oh Lucky! Time's running out for us.

'Who left the kitchen in this state! . . . Just look at the mess on the floor, flour, treacle all over the place . . . what a waste! Is this your idea of a joke, Dorrie Goodman?'

'No, Mrs Spear,' says the girl, as she rolls out the pastry for the third time. Once again it crumbles and splits. The urge to fling it across the room is overwhelming. Her hands are far too hot and sticky; a note from Lucky burns a hole in her pocket but there is no time to read it in private.

Connie is on the warpath again, picking fault with her staff, blaming them for it all as usual. 'It must be her upstairs, up to her old tricks again . . . just wait till I tell her ladyship . . . the flour fairy's been at Ruby Greville's Cordial again . . . I can smell it. You can fuel a Spitfire off one of them bottles.'

For once this slander is overheard. The Prin forgets her discretion in the rush to defend herself. 'It not me, it Meez Morton . . . she work late last night, she very naughty lady. I come in from ze pictures. I see cellar door open . . . I tell you, they rabbiting all night . . . such a racket I no sleep. You all hear siren last night, we called out by zat nasty fireman. I come down ze stairs, wiz curling rags and hot water bottle. She come out of cellar, wiz Digger man and tin of treacle . . . it everywhere, she plastered like cat wiz cream . . . very happy lady now!'

'What a cock and bull story, indeed. I have to hand it to you. You lie like a trooper . . . can't half spice up a story . . . canoodling in that damp, dark place . . . whatever next?'

'Is true . . . if no believe me, ask Meez Morton. She make this mess. If bomb fall, we find them melted like toasted sandwich . . . I tell you.' Prin spits out her false teeth in the effort.

Dorrie's eyebrows signal to Wyn in disbelief at the thought of anyone that old doing such things in the cellar.

Her employer, as if on cue, breezes through the door breathlessly. 'Sorry I'm late, girls, had a bit of a disturbed night. Oh dear . . . I must have got carried away with my baking in the blackout! We'll just do spam fritters today. Come on, chop, chop.' She pauses, seeing the shocked row of faces and gaping mouths. 'Let's get the batter a bit crisper, Connie, than last time. It was like shoe leather. If the hens are doing their bit, then let's do those eggs justice, eh?'

Dorrie notices the treacle stains on her skirt and muffles her giggles into the mixing bowl. 'Shall I fetch a mop and bucket?' she croaks. Life at the Vic was certainly taking a turn for the better!

Saturday Afternoon

Isobel Morton inspected the communal garden in front of her cottage in Vicar's Close with disgust. It had a definite morning after a night on the tiles look: battered seedy perennials collapsing like drunken soldiers and a lawn unshaven for weeks. Standards were slipping, even the autumn garden reflected her decrepitude, willing enough spirit but oh! the weak, weak flesh.

The coming visitation tolled like a knell in her head. Like a boulder thrown in a pond, Dorrie Goodman was stirring up the mud.

She cleared out the last stragglers in the clay pots by her porch and cuffed a few of the borders half-heartedly about the ears. 'My gardening days are over. There was a time I could winter dig an allotment and think nothing of it,' she sighed.

Suddenly she saw Digger Carstairs in his leather jerkin and flying boots, scattering clods of weeds in all directions like Crocodile Dundee. That was who he looked like, Crocodile Dundee, without the muscles.

'None of them knew how much of myself I put into that café. How much I nurtured it, cherished it like a baby; nothing was too much trouble. But it was no substitute for real flesh and blood and Digger was certainly that.'

March 1944

'Behold it cometh,' shouts Belle, pointing to a boy wheeling a barrow of steaming manure, wobbling like a drunken navvy.

Sid Sperrin, eleven going on seventy, with ears like jug handles and a helmet of tufted black hair, has kept his promise to deliver horse manure at a tanner a bucket to the allotment, for the Cub Scouts Spitfire campaign.

'Here, mister, 'eard the one about Utility knickers,' he pauses for their attention. 'One Yank and they're off! Get it?'

'Sid Sperrin, if your aunties hear your sauce, you'll be on that bus back to Birmingham, faster than a V1 rocket,' warns Belle.

'Nah . . . they's all deaf,' he quips. 'What they dain't hear, dain't trouble them.' He turns to Digger. 'Got any souvenirs, mister, shrapnel . . . so I can swop.'

Digger fishes in his pocket for a packet of fruit gums and some cash.

'Thanks, tah for now . . . toodle pip,' says the boy, trundling his load to his next customer.

'No flies on him,' laughs the airman, as he forks in the muck. 'How will a kid like that settle down after the war is over?'

'I wonder how any of us will be the same after five years of all this,' is the woman's reply.

Digger watches a handful of planes circling the nearby airfield, his expression distracted. 'Just look at those poor buggers trying to keep themselves from pranging each other. I'll give 'em two ops if they're lucky . . . lads out of short pants, that's what we're left with . . . schoolboys. Breaks yer bleedin' heart.'

Belle watches him tense like a coiled spring. However much she keeps him busy, amused or entertained, his eyes are always searching the sky, his ears listening for the bombers' return overhead. She lifts her spade and jabs into the claggy soil with a sigh.

Later, after closing time, Digger aims his cap at the coatstand and wings it onto the hook with unfailing accuracy. He waits discreetly until the waitresses have swept and mopped the floors, tidied out the ashtrays and fireplace, tucked all the kitchen paraphernalia to bed; until all the hundreds of menial tasks the women do each evening, before scuttling home to egg and chips or a date at the picture house, are done. That is when Belle feels loneliest of all, in the quiet kitchen, with only dish mops and tea towels for company. Then the bell rings twice and he does his trick, waltzes her around the dining room, until she feels dizzy and plonks her down in a chair to deliver a smacker, somewhere in the general direction of her lips.

'For a navigator, your aim is rotten,' she laughs.

'Near enough, I reckon, you old fusspot.' He is always tanked up, his grey eyes brittle as slate, cheeks flushed, with tiny veins like routes on a map. Stale ale and cigarettes are not the best aphrodisiac but it beats Lysol and Vim anytime.

'Where shall we go tonight?' he demands. 'Your place or mine?' They laugh, remembering the débâcle in the cellar, the shocked faces of the Prin and the staff.

'My back is giving me jip, after all that digging this afternoon,' moans the cook. Tonight they will go to her flat in Beacon Street, creep up the stairs to the first floor apartment, risk the twitching curtains, for the privacy of her three rooms. 'Not much to show for a life is it?' she had apologised the first time, as she closed the blackouts and switched on the dingy lamp.

The shabby room shimmered with faded furniture and worn linoleum flooring. All Belle's funds are sunk in the Vic, not in her wardrobe or furnishings. Digger flops down on the sofa, roots in his greatcoat for a bottle and a packet of ciggies, making himself at home. Sometimes Belle catches him staring into the gas fire, watching the flames, his eyes far away. A curtain of steel encloses him, cutting her out from any further conversation.

Her turn will come later, much later, in the middle of the night when he screams out, 'Skip! Bail out . . . Skip! Jeez move, Christ look at his face . . . his eyes. I can't find his eyes. Aw. Jeez . . . I can't . . . can't.' He wakes screaming, thrashing through the sheets. 'Get out! Bail out!'

'Shush . . . it's only a dream, shush . . .' He cannot hear at first, in that far off unspeakable world of flying metal coffins and ack-ack. The horrors he endures there are not for the conscious mind to recall. It is then that she holds him and nurses his fear, strokes and comforts that frightened child, lets him nuzzle her breast, suckle her until her nipples are hard as buttons. He feels for her body in the darkness and covers it with his own but rarely comes in climax. Belle does not mind much. Being nursemaid to his terror is enough. He cannot help himself. This need for her soothes an aching heart. For the first time in her life, she is wanted, caressed, sexed and satisfied. He wakes and reaches for a cigarette. She makes a cup of tea.

'I'm going back on ops, love. Got a posting.' She gulps back the tears.

'Surely you've done your whack . . . why volunteer for more?'

'Someone has to show those schoolboys how to duck and dive. I can't keep training them and not be man enough to go up there with them. I can't stand being grounded. Women can't understand.'

'Can't we? . . . I see what it does to you. I see the sweats, the shakes, the nightmares.'

'That's only cos I'm not up there, in control. I feel like a conchie stuck on that tarmac . . . I have to go back.'

'No one's stopping you, mate,' she replies, with a heavy heart, watching the dawn light sneak under the curtain, snuggling into the curve of his body for warmth. 'If this is all there is for me, it will do for now.'

Saturday Afternoon

Isobel felt knee joints stiffen and click, legs ache in protest at her effort. The afternoon sun was too watery to warm her thin blood. She sat on a stool, admiring the outdoor housework.

'In the beginning I loved every minute of the Victory Café; all my win-the-war cookery campaigns and daft schemes. Then came Digger halfway across the world to make a woman of me at last, to shore up the gaps for a while, a wonderful distraction, a dizzy darling of a man.

'"You only come round once, girl, so enjoy yerself. Who knows what tomorrow will bring?"

'We dug into those drunken moments, savoured the taste of loving, but the little we had was never enough. It was tiring being nursemaid to his nightmares. Silly how I thought sex would be the answer. I need a stiff gin!' She gathered up the tools, nodding her head tiredly. 'That will have to do. I don't suppose she'll even notice.'

Saturday Evening

Dorrie sat on a bench in the sunken Remembrance Garden, listening to the roar of the Saturday traffic, heading home to Match Of The Day and Bruce Forsyth.

'We are strangers to each other, Lichfield and me, like old friends grown apart with no point of contact now. Where is the spirit of the place I once knew?'

A tramp had already spread out his sleeping bag for the night, eyeing her with suspicion as she rose to place a bunch of red carnations on the marble flagstone. She fingered old poppy wreaths and read their rain-spattered messages, bleached under plastic.

She listed long forgotten names from schooldays, etched in gold on the slate memorial wall, pausing only at Solomon's precious name, bending to the little crosses; the most personal of all tokens to the fallen. Soon they would be replaced again, for the Armistice ceremonials.

'This is where I belong, alongside old pals, just another casualty of war . . . I suppose their sacrifice was worthwhile. It makes me boil

to know how much we were fobbed off with half truths and propaganda. We were all so gullible, patriotic, generous with children's lives. Now us oldies are not safe alone in the streets.'

She felt the dampness numbing her toes and stamped her feet. Twilight shadows held no fears. There was no birdsong; only the chimes of a church clock, to jolt her back again into the final remembering.

3

DANCING AT THE VIC

<u>Menu</u>

Parsnip, Leek and Bean Soup flavoured with Fennel Seeds

Lamb Chops with Rosemary and Spring Onions or Welsh Pork

Rhubarb Cobbler with Custard

March 1944

Maggie Preece sits in the window of the Vic, puffing hard on her last cigarette, savouring each drag. 'Yer dad's on the warpath again, Dorrie, hoverin' over Beacon Park, shining his torch in the bushes after dusk. Them Yanks bin at the flowerbeds again, he says, givin' the park keeper the third degree. He roots in the Air Raid Shelters . . . in all the love holes. He knows them all. Likes to catch them pants down, hard at it . . . if you catch my drift.' She pauses for her shocked audience to sit down and continues. 'Marvin . . . you will take me home to Idaho.' She mimics. 'Sure thing, hon, but shift yer skirt up a bit more.' Then up pops P.C. Plod, like the Angel Gabriel, to put the fear of God into the couple, with his one-man Crusade. I'm telling you, if the fellas ever catch him again, he'll be singing soprano. They've even got the local lads on the lookout . . . blanket watching. Allied co-operation at last! . . . what a carry on! Bribing Boy

Scouts to blow their whistles for a pocket of change or a candy bar. I bet Sid Sperrin's getting an education he'll not find in any school books! So don't do any courtin' in the city. It's not safe. He'd have you on a charge as soon as look at you. Sorry, I know he's yer dad.'

'He'd kill me, drag me to the pulpit as a fallen woman, daughter or not,' whispers Dorrie, her eyes ballooning at the very thought. 'That's not the only co-operating going on. I've heard the boys from the Base are parking trucks carelessly . . . doors unlocked while they wet their whistles . . . just time for a few locals, mention no names and I'll tell you no lies, to help themselves . . . tins, tyres. If it's not tied down it walks. Labels ripped off. Lucky says the warehouses are always losing spare parts; no one seems to care.'

'Tell Lucky boyo to keep his trap shut,' Maggie mouths.

'But it's not fair. Here we are, all doing without, while others cheat and mark down sugar as scrubbing brushes. Belle is ever so strict.' Dorrie hesitates, remembering how the search for the blue pudding was bringing temptation even to their door.

It is Chad Dixon who delivers the solution, plonking three huge cans on the kitchen table that very evening. 'There, Belladonna. That will solve your problem.' The labels read: Blueberries in Syrup. 'What can be more American than blueberry pie?'

'But I can't, Chad. Thanks. You've all been so generous.' Belle wipes floury hands on her apron and fingers the tins like crystal.

'Nonsense, lady. You have given us real hospitality. So we's payin' you back, our style, while we can . . . who knows where we'll be soon.'

That puts a different perspective on the deal, Belle figures, telling him all about her Victory Pie Menu and about her Boston beans in spicy sauce.

'Say, you're gonna need a real southern sauce, like we puts over charcoal grilled steaks!' He sees the look of disbelief on their hungry faces and laughs. 'Just you guys wait. I got a great idea. Give us the kitchen for the night and we'll dish you out the best steaks this side of Texas. Come on, boys. We've got work to do . . . sweeten up the cookhouse, boys. We'll show these fine ladies some real American chow!'

On the next Saturday night, the waitresses chivvy up any lingering customers, closing the café door promptly, drawing the blackouts onto the Square, while Chad, Abe and Lucky take over the kitchen. From under their greatcoats emerge tins of sauces, steaks the size of rabbits, real butter and a tub of almost liquid ice cream. They push the dining tables together, light candles and set the table for the feast. After a glass of hoarded sherry, they settle down to the sampling of rye whisky, root beer and soda pop.

The aroma wafting from the kitchen whets appetites better than any aperitif, rising up the stairway into the Prin's open door. She sidles down, her panda eyes peering nosily over the bannister. 'Vous eat wizout me? . . . bad boys.'

'No sweat, princess . . . there's enough sauce for the whole damn street in the back.'

'Pity Mrs Spear's not here to share it,' Belle adds half-heartedly.

Connie had sent a message that she had 'one of her backs'. Dorrie puzzles how being a martyr to her back so often coincided with the charabanc outings of the Women's Bright Hour at the Chapel.

They spin out the dinner to last all evening, savouring the warmth of their friendship, the secrecy, relishing the tastes of long-forgotten treats: the smell of fresh coffee, cigars; nectar to starved nostrils. Dorrie feels the hard liquor turning her legs to jelly and her head to cotton wool, as the booze winds its way around the table, slurring speech turning up the volume to a raucous happy sound. They spill out into the yard on the spring evening. Belle tunes the wireless to music on the Forces waveband. They jitterbug and jive to the Big Band rhythm, under a starlit sky.

'I'm dancin' with my baby.' Lucky twirls his girl on the flagstones. 'Cassie in the starlight . . . that's you, honey.'

Their noise, however, does not go unnoticed. Suddenly a

loud banging on the front door interrupts the party and familiar voices holler through the letter box.

'There's a bleedin' light full on upstairs . . . don't you know there's a war on! Stop that racket!'

Dorrie freezes to the spot at the sound of Constable Goodman's wrath. 'God help me if he finds me here, Lucky. I must disappear.' There is no escape, the wall's too high to scale and no back exit either.

'Quick . . . wiz me, up ze stairs! You two up . . . quick,' Prin comes to the rescue.

They race up the wooden stairs, past the first floor living rooms to the attic bedrooms, once servant quarters in the old house. They hide in a little bedroom with windows blacked with paint, a dismal space with bare boards and a brass bed. The constable bawls at the assembly like naughty children. The Prin whines her apology and wails her anguish, like a prima donna. 'It all my fault . . . I forget. I zink I smell the burnings . . . I fire watching . . . I getting old and forgetful.'

'This isn't the first time this old biddy's had a warning. Do you think she's signalling up there?' argues the Air Raid Warden in all seriousness. 'These foreigners!' The police-man shakes his head and surveys the scene carefully. 'Do you hold a licence for hard liquor, Mrs Morton?'

'No, no this is a private party, I can assure you.'

'And these foodstuffs . . . all presents are they?'

'Of course.'

'For services rendered?' His tone bristles with disapproval as he looks the soldiers up and down.

'I can explain, sir.' Chad intervenes. 'We owe this lady for her hospitality. We wanted to return the honour. Didn't we?' Abe nods.

'Oh yes, you lot are very generous with all your favours. I am surprised to see you here, Wyn Preece. I'm glad Dorcas isn't mixed up in this . . . shindig. I can see two other places . . . who else is here.'

'No one, some guys left early. We're going to wash up now,' Belle replies.

'I hope your passes are in order, there are enough rowdies on the street without you adding your dollar's worth.' He lingers as the men collect coats and caps and escorts them onto the street, slamming the door behind them with a flourish.

'Little Hitler!' yells the Prin, as she collects the dirty plates from the tables.

Once the danger is over, quietness descends upon the café like a soft blanket, muffling sound, soothing shattered nerve endings. Lucky and Dorrie sit on the bedstead, with hands firm on the mattress, eyes down shyly, waiting for the All Clear. Prin's voice floats up from her living room.

'Is all right, darlinks, but you stay there . . . till horrid Hitler go away, I keep watch out of the window.'

Dancing at the Victory Café

For Dorrie and Lucky, in love, alone, in hiding, there is only one place to find warmth and comfort. Here at last is a safe place for them to express all they feel in the most physical of ways. Only one thing left to do and they do it, over and over again.

In the early hours of Sunday morning, Dorrie creeps through the darkened streets, down the winding alley, letting herself into the cottage by the back door key. The reception party is waiting.

'Where have you been 'til this time of night? Answer me!' screams her mother.

'Out,' she replies.

'So we noticed. Answer your mother properly, Dorcas,' the policeman spits, the veins on his temple bulging, pulsating with rage.

'I have been out with my friends.'

'You've been in that café . . . canoodlin', making a whore of yourself with your chocolate soldier boyfriend. I can smell it on you.'

'So what if I do have a boyfriend!'

'There, Mother, what did I tell you . . . that Yankee Sergeant did warn me. She's been deceiving us with her lies . . . the Jezebel!'

'Calm yourself, Father, Dorcas will explain. It's nearly morning and we've been worried stiff. How could you? . . . dancing, smoking, drinking in such company!'

'What if I was . . . it's none of your business!' Dorrie stands firm.

'I'll give you none of our business. I am your father and you do what I say in this house.' He moves forward, raising his fist over her.

The girl jumps backwards to the door. 'Oh no you don't . . . none of that or else I'll be telling Pastor Gillibrand and your precious fellowship of believers just what an evil man you are!'

'Dorcas!' Her mother collapses on the leather armchair, clutching her chest for breath. 'Please stop this disobedience, for my sake.'

The anger is in full flood: all the years of petty restrictions, years of tyranny, years of docile obedience evaporate in the steam heat of her fury.

'Mother, do you realise what a laughing stock we are. My father creeps around Lichfield like a Peeping Tom, spying on courting couples. The soldiers know all about him and the Boy Scouts and half the city, so don't be surprised if he comes home one night black and blue. Do you think the Pastor will condone such a hypocrite as an Elder . . . a man who beats his wife and daughter to get his own way, a man who hides lead marbles in his clean white gloves, to cuff his victims round the ears more efficiently . . . like a dictator, our own little Hitler. We've put up with it far too long and I've had enough. I am off and never coming back until you both make my friend, Lucky Gordon, welcome in this house, like a son.'

'We don't believe in mixing what the Lord made separate, Dorcas.'

The policeman shakes his head, unable to master this new attack. 'If you leave this house, you can shake the dust off your feet. You will never cross this threshold, while I am alive. That right, Mother?'

Alice Goodman bows her head and prays silently, while the girl storms up to her room and flings clothes and music scores into a suitcase. She pauses at the front door, 'Goodbye then, Mam!'

'Dorrie, love, do as your father says . . . please.'

'No, Mam, I can't, not for you or anyone. He is so wrong.'

'Where will you go?'

'Somewhere I can get more love and understanding than I ever got in this hellhole. Anyway I'm joining up. It's about time I stopped hanging around. The war won't last for ever.'

The mother reaches out one last time but Joby Goodman pulls her back. 'Alice, just show her the door. I don't want to see her face again. She will bring shame on this house.'

'Don't worry, Father, I'll never bother you again but you'll regret those words when I'm famous!' She bangs the door shut with trembling hands and struggles back to Dam

Street in tears, throwing pebbles high up to the attic, until Prin unbolts the front door.

'Who ziz, at this hour?'

'It's Dorrie on the doorstep. You have a billet for the duration?'

'I 'av?' Prin rubs her bleary ears.

'You 'av,' says Dorrie, bursting into a howl of relief.

After a cup of strong tea and a face wash, she peers anxiously through the cracked mirror in the bathroom at the pale face and smiles. 'I may not look any different, but Dorcas Prudence Goodman, you're a real woman now.'

Connie can smell the afterglow of conspiracy in the restaurant; the lingering aroma of cigars and booze, a whiff of real coffee. 'Has that woman been at it in the cellar again, with the airman, using the place as a . . .' she cannot bear to say the word. 'If those Greville sisters knew what a hussy . . . how she's ruined their genteel establishment, turned it upside down and now she brings men in after hours. What's been going on, Dorrie, behind my back?'

'Belle had a bit of a do, a few friends to supper that's all.'

'Oh, yes . . . you as well? And Wyn . . . behind my back! After all I've done for this place. Not good enough now, to be invited then am I? That's the last straw. I'm not putting up with this sort of treatment!'

'Give it a rest, Mrs Spear. It was only Chad and his friends, you can't stand them anyway,' Dorrie says boldly.

'Was 'er upstairs invited?'

'She came down, yes . . . she always does . . . you know Prin.'

'Yes, like a vulture at a carcass, greedy little pig, sneaking in, stealing left overs.'

'You don't begrudge her a few bits?' Dorrie pleads.

'Never mind a few bits . . . look at this, steak gristle if I'm not mistaken. That never came off no butcher's cart . . . black market eh? Tins, too. We all know where these'll be found . . . not three miles up the Tamworth road.'

It is the empty tub of ice cream that fuels her righteous indignation into a blazing furore. 'You mean buggers, you never even left me a teaspoonful. Is this all the thanks I get . . . Well that's definitely that.' Connie tears off her pinny and storms out to see her employer, who is changing the till roll in the dining room. 'I gather there was a party here and no one thought to invite me.'

'It was all very impromptu, Mrs Spear.'

'Impromptu, my Aunt Fanny. It was planned for weeks, on the very night I am laid low. Don't say another word. I hand in my notice, as of now. I'm not going to be insulted by the likes of you.'

'Come on, Connie, don't get it all out of proportion.' Belle goes through the motions, keeping her voice tight and low.

'Don't you get uppity with me, lass. I was here long before you knew what a knife and fork were for. I know your sort: all fancy ideas and no sense. You've ruined this place. We used to have real class in here, not the riffraff you encourage, darkies, drunks.' Out pours all the wrath Connie has nursed for months.

'That's enough, Mrs Spear, we have customers!' Belle's face is flushing, her eyes sharpen and glint, lips taut and puckered.

'Do you call this lot customers? I call them floozies . . . fly by nights, Yank bashers and black marketeers!'

'Leave this minute, Mrs Spear. I won't have my diners insulted by a cantankerous, mealy mouthed sluggard, who wouldn't know quality cooking if it walked up and bit her. You're sacked!'

'Don't worry, I'm off. Good riddance to bad rubbish . . . to all of you!' the manageress shouts. 'And I'll make damn sure people know what sort of tricks go on in this dump!' She flounces through the door with a flourish. Only the clink of morning coffee cups rattle in the restaurant. The silence is deafening.

'That's the best morning's work I've done in years,' says Belle as she breezes into the back.

'I'm not so sure,' whispers Dorrie, as she buries her head in the mixing bowl. Wyn drops her tray and snivels into the sink.

May 1944

On the day of the military parade, flags are flying at the Vic. Dorrie has been up since dawn, mixing ingredients for the tray bakes, while Belle puts the finishing touches to their display. VICTORY TO OUR GALLANT ALLIES, bedecked with bunting and Union Jacks in the window. Prin has been bribed into polishing the knives and forks while Wyn attempts a patriotic floral table piece, which will not stay upright.

It is Judgement Day for the Vic, when all their efforts will be marked for originality, style and taste. The café buzzes with excitement. Belle darts from front to back, checking, cross checking. As Connie's dramatic exit and the arrival of Dorrie upstairs coincided, it was easier to employ the girl full time until her call-up day arrived. Dorrie is praying that her scones will do the baker justice for once and not shrivel into pebbles. She has been far too busy to dwell on the change in her circumstances. For the first time in her life, she feels freedom rising like sap through the stem, a blossoming of options instead of restrictions. She plans at long last to sing with the Five Aces Showband at the very next opportunity.

Bindy Baverstock pops down from the Cathedral Close with her young daughter, clutching a bunch of spring flowers, to give the café a final once over. 'You must win. You've certainly captured the spirit of the competition. I've heard it's been a pretty poor show so far. Have you heard the rumours? The big push is coming soon. Then we really will have something to celebrate!'

For once even Wyn manages to look smart, her lace cap hiding the worst of her Amami permanent wave, which frizzles around her head like a thrush's nest, much to Dorrie's horror. In the excitement of putting on the solution over curling pins in the blackout, they had cooked the curls into corkscrews.

'Why can't I have beautiful locks like yours, instead of this mousey fluff?' Wyn moans.

'You'd soon get fed up with being called carrot top and copper knob. It has a will of its own.' Dorrie points to the wispy tendrils escaping from her cap. 'I wish mine was like Mrs Morton's . . . all straight and smooth.'

The girls peer out onto the Square for the arrival of the judges. The streets bristle with troops and onlookers, waiting for the parades to start and the fairground to open, where polished guns line up alongside the recruitment tents and rifle ranges in the park.

The Civic dignitaries in scarlet robes and tricorn hats are marshalled outside the Guild Hall to inspect the American guard. They salute the march past in the drizzle. Dorrie is keen to see the jazz bands who have marched from their barracks to the city for the occasion. Belle is too keyed up herself to let them dart onto the pavement for more than a second or two. 'Can you see anyone we know?' she asks.

'Only Curtis Jackson, the M.P. and that awful McCoy patrolling the pavements.' Dorrie has not seen Lucky for a week. He had not shown up at their usual rendezvous under the railway arch and she worries at his absence.

The lunchtime rush is long over. The Victory pies sag half eaten, crumbs and spillage hastily mopped up, the Bortsch soup sits lukewarm on the stove. At four o'clock, two men in gaberdine macintoshes and trilby hats come through the door, officials from the Council and their long awaited performance begins. The men want to speak to Belle in private. She takes them into the kitchen for a minute, then shows them politely to the door.

'That was quick!' says Wyn, looking puzzled.

One look at the cook's white face tells a sorry tale. 'All that bloody work . . . for nothing. I can't believe it. I wish Digger was here.' She is close to tears.

'What's happened?' they whisper, as she ushers them into the back.

'We've been disqualified!'

They gasp. 'Whatever for?'

'Apparently we contravened the regulations. It has come to their notice that we've been using ingredients not acquired through the proper channels!'

'What ingredients?'

'The blasted blueberries . . . and the tins of molasses for the bean bake. All the stuff Chad and Lucky gave us, as their hospitality rations. They said it was black marketeering. Of course, I had no receipts either. Someone wrote to the Council, saying we are not playing fair . . . someone wrote a complaint. Who would be mean enough to do that to us, do you think?'

'Connie Spear,' they chorus in unison.

'That's right . . . a former employee of the Victory Café took it upon herself to let it be known that she could not be a party to our fraudulent entry . . . et cetera!'

Suddenly the spring day lies in tatters around them. They stand shell shocked, flattened and disappointed. Dorrie has no heart now to follow the crowds to the park. Belle crumples onto a chair, sups tea and stuffs her face with blueberry pie. 'I feel so insulted, I do my best to bring some imagination into my menu . . . to brighten up the stodge with a bit of flair! What's the point! We might as well dish up lentil sausage and gravy browning, prunes and custard. No one cares about real food any more . . . I think I shall swallow a bottle of Ruby Greville's revenge and get blotto.'

She is missing Digger Carstairs, who is now somewhere in Lincolnshire, back on a tour of night ops, they were told. More worrying for Dorrie is the absence of Lucky and his gang and she fears their unit has been posted south suddenly. On the mantelpiece in the flat lies the envelope containing her own call up papers. Soon she, too, will leave the city and the precious hours to this departure are now ticking away.

At first, Dorrie thinks it is the wind rattling the window above her camp bed in Prin's living room. But the night is calm. Then she recognises the tap of stones against the glass. In a daze, she pulls back the blackout curtains. A figure is lurking in the doorway of the department store across the street. For a moment she freezes in fear as her movements are seen and the figure darts out. It is Lucky. Dorrie creeps down the stairs, sussing the boards carefully, loosens the bolts and pulls him through the door. 'Lucky . . . what on earth are you doing?'

He is shaking, his dirty uniform torn. 'I gone A.W.O.L. honey . . . I had to . . . I can't stand no more. I bin framed for sumptin' I ain't done, so I ain't hangin' around.'

Dorrie guides him upstairs. 'Come on, let me put the kettle on.'

'What is it with that McCoy? He hate my guts. I swear I ain't done nuttin' but he done for me this time,' the soldier gasps.

'Slow down, cool it as you say,' murmurs Dorrie as she closes out the night and lights an oil lamp. Only then does she see the plum coloured bruising on his face.

'I just got the hell out . . . you knows I drive trucks all over supplying bases, the trucks is filled with stuff. I don't know what and I don't care. Two days ago I was told to get this load down to Worcester. Me and Abe, we's cruisin' down the highway, when I sees this jeep full of Snowdrops followin' . . . flaggin' us down. No problem, we reckon, so I gets out to see what they want. They say all the stuff is stolen . . . that ma papers ain't okay. That we is stealing the goddam truck . . . would you believe, Jeez. I tell them they is talkin' chickenshit . . . so they beat the hell out of us both, right there on the sidewalk, in front of folks and chuck us in the back of the truck. So I waits till I get some breath and jump out the back. Abe was too beat to move. We was not handcuffed together. I reckon they think we is out cold. I hitch my way back in the dark.'

'Oh Lucky, you should have gone south.'

'I was coming back to see you. I knows Prinny will not turn me over . . . but to find you here too . . . come away with me, honey . . . we'll go to Ireland . . . let's beat it, honey, away from this war. It ain't ma business anymore.'

'If you're innocent, give yourself up.'

'Never . . . they'll shoot me.'

'For a few tyres?'

'Stealing from Uncle Sam is a shootin' offence. This Colonel is a mean guy . . . he's shot men for less.'

'But you did nothing but your job.'

'I can't prove it. We is dead meat. Come with me now . . . please, honey.' Lucky paces the floor, pleading.

'Hang on . . . you can stay here in hiding . . . I'll talk Prin round. Chad will help us . . . I'll talk to him. No one need know you're here.'

'No, Dorrie, don't tell a soul . . . I'll keep runnin'. The sooner I go the safer for you.'

'No . . . stay here, rest. If you are innocent, someone has to plead your case and clear your name. Don't give up yet for our sakes.'

'Honey, you don't understand Jim Crow. It one law for whiteys, another for the black man. Believe me there's no justice waitin' for me in that camp.'

'There has to be, Lucky. This is England. Surely someone can help us?' In the darkness, they cling together like frightened children, waiting for the dawn.

The following night, Dorrie pedals furiously out of the city at dusk, risking life and limb on the narrow winding lanes; over the humpy canal bridges; through hamlets of red bricked cottages, onwards to the scrublands of the open Heath. As she approaches the Barracks, a gaggle of giggling girls with ankle-strapped high heels and jaunty swagger coats tumble out of a lorry, waddling and wobbling along the rough track towards the perimeter fence of the camp, under cover of copse and shrubs. Grateful for the anonymity of their company, she wheels the bike onto the verge, while they stand around smoking, adjusting their stocking seams and elaborate pompadour hairstyles, powdering noses and ducking out of searchlights. They stare at her coldly.

'What you playing at . . . sod off. This is our patch,' spits a hoyden, plastered in panstick, as she stubs out her fag on a thick platformed sole.

'I'm only trying to contact a friend.' Dorrie smiles innocently.

'Oh yeah? We've all got friends here . . . very friendly aren't we, Peg?' answers an older woman, with a thick Black Country accent. She observes Dorrie's plain skirt and tweed jacket; her homespun manner. 'Are you Welfare? Come to spy on us . . . get us sent to Homes for Wayward girls, all locked up, Miss Bobby Socks. Cos if you are . . .' Threats are in the air.

'No . . . do I look like Welfare? I have to get a message to a friend, that's all. Where are you from?'

'Never you mind . . . far enough to need a bleedin' taxi . . . too far for Shanks's pony. We can scarper sharp enough if them do-gooders try and spoil the party. They sneak up in vans and cop you doin' yer business. We're only giving lonely boys a service . . . perform tricks through the wire fence if we have to.'

Dorrie tries not to look shocked. 'It must be very risky.'

'We can take care of ourselves. Can't we, girls.' She produces a small packet from her purse. 'See!'

'What's in there?' Dorrie asks.

'Hark to Miss Innocent. Haven't you seen a french letter before?' The woman blows one up like a balloon and fixes it to the fence. 'X marks the spot.' They cackle like geese, pulling a concealed flap cut in the wire . . . a well-trodden entrance to the rows of Quonset huts.

Dorrie hangs back, suddenly afraid.

'Are you coming or not? Miss Goody Two Shoes?'

She crawls under the wire with shaking limbs. It's now or never. The girls shine a torch along the path. In the distance, the muffled sound of Glen Miller on a wireless: the jaunty rhythm of Little Brown Jug warms the air. The women seem to know the layout of huts, opening a barracks door noisily. The men lounging on bunks casually inspect the night's contingent of girls for sale.

'Where's yer jungle juice, fellas,' yells a blonde in skimpy red skirt and real nylon stockings, with seams running up her leg, like the rocky road to Dublin. 'Come on, we ain't got all night.'

Dorrie searches desperately to see if she can recognise a familiar black face, but they are newly arrived recruits. She braves their obvious interest. 'Sorry to spoil the party, folks, but I'm looking for Private Chad Dixon from Philadelphia, friend of Lucky Gordon, drummer in the Five Aces Showband.'

'Are you now . . . well we's all Luckies here. Take your pick . . . it's your lucky night, catch ma drift,' is the only reply.

'No . . . not tonight, I got to see Chad. It's urgent. He's a sort of preacher man.'

'Oh naughty, naughty . . . little sweetie. We don't want no preacher's kickin' ass in this joint.'

'Please, you've got to help.'

'Look you is holdin' up the show. Get out . . . shoot or we'll make a meal of you, babe.'

Dorrie heads out of the door and into the darkness. The camp tracks confuse her. Aware only that she is now on enemy territory, she slides under hut windows, peers through open doors, panic rising with each yard further into the Base. If only she knew where to look. Suddenly she sees a group of familiar faces, some of the regulars who frequent the Vic, and calls out, accosting them with the beam of her torch. 'Stubby, Tex . . . shsh! It's me, Lucky's Dorrie, from the Vic . . . shsh! Over here. Lucky's in trouble. I must see Chad. Please help me,' she cries, seeing their startled expressions.

Stubby searches blindly for the disembodied voice. 'Dorrie, is it really you? Don't move a muscle, stay put. Keep down. There's a lot of traffic on this track . . . I see what I can do.'

She needs no encouragement to crouch in the darkness, the spring night is chilly and a wind from the east whips across the bleak Common straight from Russia. Eventually, she hears footsteps scrunching on the asphalt and then a pause.

'You got Lucky with you, Dorrie?' whispers the soft drawl of Chad Dixon.

'No. He won't come. Says he'll not get a fair hearing.'

'It's a bad business, Dorrie, if he deserts. Big trouble, honey.'

'He didn't do it.'

'I knows, you knows but this Colonel is so unpredictable. It's bad for morale.'

'He was set up by McCoy,' she says. 'Please come and talk to him. He's going crazy. How's Abe?'

'In the jailhouse . . . out cold, real bad. You gotta make him give himself up, child. They'll come lookin'.'

'Then we'll go to Ireland, run away together. No one will find us there.'

'Don't be stupid. They watch the ports. You two'll stick out a mile. Go back, Dorrie. It's far too dangerous for you here. I'll do what I can . . . speak to the Pastor. Somptin' nasty's going on here and it don't smell good.'

'Lucky says he got his orders from a guy he'd never seen before.'

'This place is burstin' with new guys. That don't mean a thing but no one knows who is who anymore.'

Chad escorts her back towards the tents where a party is in full swing. The girls are plying their trade from tent to tent. 'Makes me real ashamed of Uncle Sam's army,' Chad whispers. 'This is what we'll be remembered for . . . sex and the jitterbug!'

'It's only a bit of fun.' Dorrie tries to soothe his embarrassment.

'No, child, it's business, hard cash. It don't do either nation proud. I wish I could escort you through the front gate, 'stead of sneakin' through the fence. I'll be prayin' for you both. Make him see sense. I'll do what I can, hurry on. God be with you.'

Someone has let her tyres down as a joke. It is a slow sad trail back to the city, eerie and cold with only the dim bicycle lamp for comfort in the gloom. Dorrie sings her repertoire of showband favourites to keep up her spirits. Lucky must see sense now. Chad will find a strong defence. The Colonel will understand the mistake. She parks the cycle by the front door. The street is silent and dark. At the end of the cobblestones stand the three spires of the Cathedral, offset against the dawning sky. Suddenly a torch flashes in her face, blinding her for a second. A hand pulls her back from the door.

'I got you both now, babe,' triumphs Sergeant Burgess McCoy. Dorrie struggles to evade his grasp but McCoy is muscle strong and she is no match for his animal cunning. He rings the bell and shouts through the letter box. 'Come out, Nigger boy, I got yer two bit whore . . . right here. Come out and get what's comin' to yer. No black boy makes a fool of Burgess McCoy and lives to tell the tale. Come on . . . nice and easy, no tricks or I'll give this little piece of white trash something to remember me by.'

The girl kicks hard as he gropes her body. 'Let me go!'

'Stay still, missy. Why you fussin' . . . what's a slice off a cut loaf. I knows you is hot for it. Redheads is always hot for it.'

Terror melts her limbs, only her scream rings out, 'Don't do this, Sergeant, please. Don't do this to us. You've no right.'

'Move once more and I'll squeeze every breath out of your whorin' body, little song bird, so you ain't going to croon no more.' She feels his thumb on her throat. 'No coon takes a breath without my permission. I gets first pickin's . . . you made a big mistake, honeybun. Now I got you both just where I wants you.'

'No you ain't.' Lucky Gordon shoots out the door like a bullet from a gun and with one spring jumps on the soldier. Dorrie sees a kitchen knife, glinting coldly in the moonlight. 'No, Lucky . . . don't kill him. He's not worth it.'

The sergeant fumbles for his holster. Dorrie's cries are drowned by the screech of brakes. Suddenly, a flash of headlights beams in on the scene, a rush of boots on the cobbles.

'Drop the knife, Gordon, cool it, McCoy,' yells an officer. Curtis Jackson moves forward pointing a gun. Chad sits helplessly in the back of the jeep.

'Let me kill the bastard now.' McCoy raises his gun. Dorrie leaps forward and shields her lover. 'Kill him and you kill me . . . an unarmed civilian. Want to hang for me, McCoy?'

'Put it down, buddy. It's over. We got our deserter. No civilians. You know the rules. We got what we came for. Shove him in the back.' McCoy hesitates, puts his gun back slowly, pushing Lucky towards the jeep. 'Let him say goodbye to his girl,' Chad yells but is ignored as they handcuff the soldier.

Dorrie runs after the jeep. 'Lucky, I'll find a way . . . you're innocent. Sergeant Jackson, help him. You got the wrong man.' The engine revs and roars off. Lucky turns his head, his eyes burning with fear. 'I love you, Lucky Gordon . . . I love you . . .' Dorrie's voice fades as she sinks onto the pavement before her only witnesses but the three silent spires stab impotently into the dawn sky.

No one can make any sense out of Dorrie's garbled tale. Prin, convinced that she was only dreaming, tries to allay her growing fears. As hours pass into days, the girl, desperate for news, makes one last stand on Lucky's behalf.

On a bright May morning with pillowy white clouds scudding across the blue sky, Dorrie struggles in the wind, uphill towards the open Heath, her hair streaming backwards like a banner. Traffic, heading south, snakes in a long grey convoy of trucks, lorries full of soldiers with gum-chewing grins, whistling their appreciation as her best skirt rides slowly up her thighs with the effort: hard evidence of rumours of a 'big push', heading troops and supplies down to the Channel ports. Oblivious of their wolf whistles, she pedals furiously to the Barrack gates, parks her bike purposefully and demands to see the officer in charge.

'Miss Goodman. I've come about the civvy job in the offices. It's all been fixed by Mrs Baverstock. Friend of the Colonel. Hurry up, I'm a bit late,' she bluffs, her legs trembling at her lies.

'Haven't I seen you before?' says the sentry, eyeing her carefully.

'Perhaps. I'm a friend of Curtis Jackson and Sergeant McCoy.' She flirts coyly. The guard makes a call and, to her amazement, lifts the barrier and lets her cycle through. Trying not to wobble, she makes for the administration block at the heart of the red bricked fortress with its turrets and crenellated splendour. One step nearer to Lucky; the thought is the only force pushing her forward. She opens a side door, asks for the Colonel's Office H.Q. trying to look official and in command of the situation. A soldier carrying boxes points her up the stairs, down a long corridor, too busy to ask for her pass. To her amazement her presence goes unchecked.

Down in the yard, she watches all the busy preparations of an army on the move, loading, lifting, reversing huge lorries out towards the main road. An officer stops her progress and commands her to sit outside his room. 'The Colonel has no appointments today. Who did you say you were told to see? Wait here on this chair. I'll make enquiries.'

She waits precisely until his back is turned, shoots through the door and turns the key, dragging the desk, chair and cabinet into a barricade. She hears him return.

'Where's that red-haired dame gone?' He turns the door knob. 'What the hell! Are you in there? Open this door!'

'Not until I see Lucky Gordon . . . I demand to see the Colonel. He is innocent!' She can hear him charging about outside, raising the alarm.

'Hellfire, we got a crazy dame in my office . . . shouting the odds about some poor guy . . . another one wanting sweets from Uncle Sam for her bastard baby. Get the M.P.s and a doctor. Who the Hell let her in?' He shouts through the door, 'Look, honey, if you come out now, you can go home, no charges, nice and peaceful.'

'I have to see the Colonel. It's about Private Charlie Gordon and the trucks. I have to make them understand . . . if you don't, I'll jump out of the window. I mean it. I was there when you took him . . . when McCoy tried to kill him. I want to know what's going on . . . Please.'

'Who is this Gordon to you then? Promised to marry you did he?'

'I tried to make him give himself up. He didn't steal any truck. He's not that kind of guy. I love him and we want to do some shows together. I promised I'd sing with the Five Aces Showband.' There is silence. Slowly, Dorrie feels a sick weariness seeping through her body. What is the point of taking on the might of the U.S.A. Armed Force?

She peers through the window to see a group of soldiers with guns looking up at her. This stupid idea was doomed to failure, a silly impulsive, childish tantrum. Now, alone and afraid, only anger fuels her resolve to help Lucky, no matter what the cost to herself. She sits under the window, curled up in a ball, trying not to cry. Someone taps on the door, a different voice calls.

'We've brought a friend of yours here to see you, Miss Goodman. Let him in.'

'Oh no, I'll not be tricked. Who is it?'

'You won't see him if you don't open the door.'

'Lucky is that you there?' Silence again.

'It's me, Chad . . . Chad Dixon, Lucky's friend. Dorrie, let me in. You won't be harmed. I promise.'

'I want to see Lucky. When I hear his voice. Then I'll open the door.'

'Honey, he ain't here, let me in and I can explain, please, Dorrie. I promise.'

Dorrie wavers for a moment. 'Where is he, Chad, what's happened? Why can't he come, Chad? Tell me. I miss him so much. We've got plans to sing in the Showband soon.' Her voice trails away into a soft moan of anguish as a searing pain encircles her gut and forces her to her knees.

'Let me in, honey, what I gotta say ain't gonna be easy and I need to hold you while I tell you.'

The furniture is dragged slowly away and the key turns in the lock. Outside the men stare at her strangely and Chad stands with eyes full of tears. But it is the way he clutches his cap that buckles her knees. He looks to the Officer, who nods as he squeezes through the door. Dorrie waits, suddenly ice cold and calm, every detail of the room crystal in clarity: the glitter of dust on the rays of sunlight, the tick of the wall clock, each second in slow motion. The pastor sits down on the floor beside her.

'There was an accident in the camp last week, Dorrie. All this business with Abe, Lucky and McCoy. Some real bad feelin' in the jailhouse when they brings in Lucky on desertion charge. It's a mean place . . . a jail full of roughnecks . . .

mean guys, who'll take on any cause to settle their own scores. They starts a hollerin' and clangin' plates, smashin' things, wrecking the joint . . . stabbed a guard and busted into the yard on a breakout.' Chad's voice begins to crack and he swallows hard. 'You have to understand, these things just happen. The guards were reinforced . . . to cool off the riot. Someone stuck a knife in McCoy's ribs, straight to his heart.'

'On no! Lucky!' Dorrie cries.

'No . . . it wasn't Lucky, not him this time, just another prisoner with a score to settle. Once the shootin' started, it was every man for himself, all runnin' for cover . . . a real mess . . . bullets flyin' . . . only Lucky gotten himself caught in the crossfire, a bullet in the back. He didn't know what hit him. I guess he just ran out of luck, honey.'

Dorrie buries her head, unable to cry. 'And it's all my fault. I should never have told anyone, if only I'd sent him packing.'

'They knew where he was, honey. McCoy had been stalking your place for days.'

'Poor Lucky. No one to protect him. He was innocent.'

'Yeah, they knows it now. When McCoy gets killed, out comes all the rats, fleein' for cover, coverin' their asses. Abe and Lucky were set up as decoys for some real stealing going on. Abe is doin' fine and is out of that jail.'

'Can I see my Lucky, then?'

'No. He ain't here no more. His folks back home'll be told in due course.'

'No inquests, no investigations, then?'

'That's none of my business, you know how it is now. If you makes a fuss, it'll all be denied. I'm so sorry.'

'So am I. I wish your rotten army never came to this place.'

'Don't be bitter, Dorrie. We can't change a thing. Come on out of here, I can get you a lift back to town. The Colonel won't press charges as long as you leave peaceful.' They stand up awkwardly. Dorrie brushes her skirt. 'I have my bike, thank you. I will manage.'

'Wish us luck, Dorrie, we is movin' soon, I reckon.'

'You don't want my luck. Look where it got Charlie. I'm bad news.'

She is cautioned and admonished, frogmarched briskly out of the Base. Dorrie mounts her bike and turns her ashen face grimly towards the city without a backward glance.

'Come away, love. Come away from the wire. They've all gone. Look, no tents, not a black face in sight . . . all gone south. Stop this torturing of yourself, Dorrie. We're worried sick about you.' Belle Morton tries to prise the girl's clawing fingers off the perimeter fence.

'He's still here. I know he is. I can hear his voice calling me. We never said goodbye. How can he go without saying goodbye. They've buried him here on the Heath. I've heard the ghost tales. I can feel him here. Lucky, where are you?' Dorrie paces the boundary banging the wire, throwing the weight of her body in vain, forcing it to yield. 'How can I bear this, never-again feeling? Come on, show me where you are!'

'Dorrie snap out of this! He's not here. He's dead. They've gone to France. Cry it out of your system. You have to let go of your grief or it will make you ill!'

'I don't care!'

Belle feels her words ricochet off a brick wall. 'Your mother called in to see you yesterday. Why won't you speak to her? She looks so concerned. Wyn's chest is very wheezy and Prin is so lost without your company. Don't shut us out. We all care about you . . . if there is anything we can do!'

Dorrie stares ahead unmoved. 'I suppose this is all a punishment for me leaving the fellowship. My father's curse on me for disobedience. My sinfulness has killed him. It should be me, not Lucky. It's not fair!'

'No, love, it ain't fair. Who ever says it is is a fool. Digger Carstairs has gone missing. I've just been told. His crew bailed out somewhere in Holland, they think. The best thing that happens to me over, poof . . . before it really began. No, life isn't bloody fair!'

'Oh, Mrs Morton, I'm sorry. I didn't realise. He was a good bloke and a laugh.' The stone wall is cracking.

'Don't give up on life now. I'm not giving up on that daft bugger yet! Not until I see him written out in black and white. You're starting a new life in the Land Army next week. Eighteen years old, with a voice like an angel and looks to match. Who knows what the future holds for you? Chop, chop. Remember Prin and her blasted teacups?' Belle sniffs through her tears. 'We all want to hear you on the wireless one day, making Lucky Gordon real proud of you. He was the first to spot your talent. Live for him!'

Droplets glisten in the dark pools of Dorrie's eyes and roll down her nose like glass beads. Belle hugs her tightly and the floodgates open.

Saturday Night

The hotel bedroom was cheerful but stuffy, the meal indifferent. Oblivious of the weekend revellers who tumbled out of the pubs, shouting and cursing across the city with noisy exuberance, Dorrie paced the city pavements briskly to ease the ache no aspirin will ever shift, circling around the floodlit Cathedral Close.

She searched the starlit sky in vain for the splutter of bombers limping home, distress flares torching their return to the anxious ground crew below. 'Lucky moon, lucky moon. Bring the boys back safely soon. Am I clinging onto the past or is the past still clinging onto me? This place keeps releasing my memories from their rusty chains. How much more can I bear? Dorrie's last stand indeed. How could I have been so naive?'

4

DORRIE. SOLO

<u>Menu</u>

Pumpkin Soup

Farmhouse Pasty with Vitamin Salad

Bakewell Tart or Summer Pudding

July 1944

Dorrie watches the procession arching slowly ahead up the field: the tanned leather backs of the 'conchies' stacking up the stooks as they laugh alongside the other Land Army women. Her own burnt flesh prickles in the heat, mite-lumps, swollen and scratched raw, sting in the sweating recesses of her groin; the itching unbearable. In the fierce heat of late July, the straw pokes needles through holes in gum boots. Her felt hat is the only protection on her neck, hot and sticky with brittle bleached tendrils of baked hair straggling across her brow. Brown freckles merge into a mottled rash across her pink face and arms. Drips of perspiration seep beneath her swollen breasts. She tastes the tang of salt on her cracked lips.

The gang of field workers follow the relentless pace of the cart horse, then break for a few minutes to sit under the cart for shade, swigging cups of elder-flower champagne from brown jugs and munching pasties brought out by one of the farmer's daughters. Dorrie as usual sits apart from the gang, lost in her own world of fury.

'Hey you. Give us a hand. Get up on that cart and sort out the bales. Come on, Marmalade, shift yer arse!' yells the farmhand in corduroy britches, tied at the knee with string, spitting green phlegm after each sentence. Dorrie rises sullenly and clambers up onto the bales. The sky spins like a carousel. 'Straighten 'em up, girl.'

She fingers the bloody remains of a rabbit sliced by the sickle, needles of straw scratching her skin. She pauses, the urge to jump and end all the shame too strong to resist. Why go on living when I am pregnant? Oh yes, for certain. No more fooling herself with the idea that a change of routine and Land Army tasks had stopped her monthlies, stemmed the flow.

The itchy breasts can no longer be ignored, the nauseating taste of tea on her tongue, the swelling lump in her abdomen. Any dullard notices such changes. No chore is too hard to try, the mucking out, lifting sacks, pulling ropes, nothing too dirty or heavy for Dorrie Goodman's tired back. She embraces her work with grim enthusiasm and a manic energy which makes her unpopular, a subject of suspicion and then indifference amongst her fellow troops. It suits her to keep herself apart.

'That'll do . . . don't make a meal of it. Come on down . . . what the bleedin' hell!' The gang master stops as the young girl flings herself onto the earth with an awesome careless leap. She lies stunned, her legs splayed but unbroken. 'You stupid cow. What yer do that for . . . could have killed someone, landin' like that . . . must be sun stroked. Get up.' It's all the sympathy she gets.

Dorrie gasps while her arms are yanked up. She is pushed under the cart in the cool, to get her breath back. Will that crazy act do the trick? She is running out of punishments to rid herself of the burden. Every whispered potion she has tried to swallow, gulping gin when she could find a bottle, until she retched and the bed swam. Fear prowls like a tiger, stalking her day and night. She funked the knitting needle cure, stabbings only remind her of Lucky and his death. As each month passes, her condition harder to conceal to a knowing eye, brings nearer the fate of a shameful discharge. Her sanity holds by the slenderest of threads. This silly impulsive gesture brings only bruises and an aching back. The unwelcome guest is determined to stay.

Haytime turns into harvest home, to ploughing and harrowing. As the autumn gales lash the fields, so Dorrie invests in baggy dungarees and keeps her secret. Away from prying eyes, surrounded by girls who think her stuck up and stand-offish, the firecracker, the snarling tiger, she conceals seven months of pregnancy. She keeps well away from Lichfield and sad memories.

The farm is high on the Derbyshire Peaks, near the market town of Ashbourne. It is natural to gravitate to the Derby Café for off-duty hours, far from the Vic. She billets herself in the Public Library to escape into books and the silence of reading rooms, avoiding concerts and dancehalls, especially the sounds of beat music. The muscles in her jaw stiffen, her mouth dries. It feels as if her throat is full of pebbles choking the breath. Dorrie no longer hums or sings to herself. Music holds no comfort for her.

Then comes the morning when she forks her toe through her one decent Wellington boot, the spike searing her flesh. Her screams bring the farmer running. His wife bundles her in a cart and trundles down to Ashbourne village to the doctor's rooms, stemming the blood with a tea cloth.

'Come on, young lady, let's have those dirty clothes off,' says the doctor.

'I'll manage as I am. It's just my foot,' she replies.

'I'll be the judge of that,' says the eagle-eyed nurse who happens to be assisting that morning. She peels off the dungarees and glances at Dorrie's swollen body. The camouflage of shirting falls away.

'How long have you been in this condition?'

'I don't know what you mean,' brazens the girl, her cheeks stinging as the foot is washed and examined. The doctor holds her gaze.

'Come on, young woman. That's no football in there. We both know you're with child.'

Such an old fashioned Bible phrase, smiles Dorrie to herself. 'With child' indeed. Little do they know how hard I've tried to be without one! The doctor peers over half moon spectacles, summons her onto the couch, covers her embarrassment with a cotton sheet and palpates the belly. 'How long since your last courses?'

'I don't know,' answers Dorrie, for once truthfully, silenced as he squeezes and defines the growing shape, taking a cold cone to her lump and listening intently.

'You'd better get yourself booked in soon, silly girl. The head is engaging. I shall have to inform the farmer of your condition, unless you do so first. In the forces is he . . . the father?'

'Lost at sea,' she lies. There is no point in telling the truth.

'You know you will be discharged . . . regulations.'

'I can take care of myself,' she croaks.

'Can you take care of a baby, though? What were you thinking of . . . there are Homes for girls like you but you've left it very late now. Go home to your parents and arrange for the baby to be taken away at birth to a good home. Throw yourself on the mercy of your parents. They usually stand by their girls,' he argues with breezy optimism.

Where do these men get such ideas? That parents like mine would condone a bastard; parents so firmly anchored to Victorian times. It's the workhouse for wayward daughters like me. She says nothing, dresses meekly, relieved in a strange way that her secret is now public. She collects forms for a change of rationbook, allows them to stitch up her wound and hobbles back to the waiting cart. Somehow, drained of energy and resolve, she brazens out the sniggering and darted, 'told you so' glances of the other women. There are no allies to support her. Her own pride and shame saw to that. Underneath lurks a terrible fear. An awesome predicament awaits her in a few weeks' time; a predicament only she alone can sort out.

It becomes the longest journey of her life, standing in the bus queue with her kit bag, waiting in the smoky terminal for a connection, her legs swollen, her stomach churning with fear. Even the newspaper barely distracts the ache in her back; with news of V2 rocket attacks and the American advances into the Moselle.

Thank goodness for the farmer's wife, a staunch Methodist who, much to her surprise, had taken pity on Dorrie's plight and allowed her to stay on as unpaid skivvy in the dairy. She had drawn the line, however, at having a bastard delivered in the house. As her time came closer, Dorrie was sent packing.

Dorrie waits until dusk to catch the bus from Derby to Lichfield City. She sits by the window, staring out into the gloom, watching breath condense on the glass like streaming tears, shutting out views of the darkening countryside, shutting in the cocoon of chattering passengers. She rubs out a clear patch, to peer up at myriads of stars, heralding a frost.

'Are you watching over me, Lucky Gordon . . . wherever you are? Can you see the mess you've landed me in? You'd better pull one out of the hat for me tonight.' She winces as the ache in her backbone gathers into a searing clinch over her stomach. The bumping charabanc jolts the seat and she curls, knees up, to ease the pain. When eventually the bus draws into Lichfield, she alights in pitch darkness, with only the bright Bomber's moon torching the towpath along the Minster pool, which nestles under the Cathedral wall. The shimmering gold disc reflecting icily on the pool. Its water is tempting but cold and not deep enough. She is too exhausted to walk the half mile to the deeper reservoir at Netherstowe.

The Vic is shuttered and closed; no telltale signs of Belle Morton working late in the back. She rings the bell, her finger sticks on the buzzer as another pain grabs at her stomach.

'Who'z zat . . . wakin' ze dead at zis hour?'

'Prin . . . Prin. It's me, Dorrie.'

'I know no Dorrie. Dorrie who? She gone away! . . . go away.'

'Let me in . . . it is Dorrie. I'm so cold. I did mean to come back but I have a good reason, please, Prin.'

The woman relents and opens the door cautiously. 'You vicked girl . . . disappear . . . poof like smoke. Not a word.' She stares at the girl. 'So it is you . . . rolling up like ze bad penny.'

'Let me in. I'm freezin' out here and wet.'

'Wet? It no raining.'

'Well I'm soaking, I'll explain everything.' Dorrie can hardly climb the stairs, her hands on the banisters clammy, her legs strangely disobedient. She feels the warm rush of water down her legs, leaving a trail of drips on the bare boards.

Prin closes the curtains and puts on the light, muttering, prattling at her arrival. 'All the soldiers gone . . . thiefs in the night . . . no rations any more. Chad write me a letter . . . poor Abe, he stood on a mine . . . no more Abe. Where you been?'

'Not now, Prin. Please God . . . I've got other things on my mind.'

'So I see, big fat cow. How long vous been like zat?'

'Not much longer . . . my waters have broken. What happens next?'

'How I know? I never have ze baby . . . go to ze hospital, chop, chop.'

'I can't, Prin, no one must know I'm here. Please help me. I can do it here.'

'You crazy lady . . . no room here for babies.'

'Just for tonight, please. I'll move on then . . . God the bloody thing's coming. I must go upstairs. Let me get rid of this thing. I want rid of it now.'

'Don't say that, Dorrie. Is it poor Lucky's?' Prin takes her arm and guides her up to the attic.

'Yes, of course, but he can't do much for me now, can he?' Dorrie fights each contraction, spitting out her anger, tensing her muscles against the pain.

'That's right! You curse like Eve . . . let it out. I make you warm.' Prin clatters down the stairs to light her burner. 'You come right place. We have lots of babies in ze street. My mamma, she go help, I know vat to do,' she shouts from the kitchen.

'God! I hope you do,' yells Dorrie. 'I hope it's not another of your porky pies.'

'I make it all right for vous . . . no worries.'

The night is one long pain, a relentless tightening and squeezing in her gut. 'How long does this take?' Dorrie cries out.

'How I know? I bring some tea.'

Dorrie is promptly sick over the linoleum. 'Sorry, I bought some chips for the journey.'

'Silly girl, you no eat when you pushing babies out.'

Perhaps Prin does know something after all. The old woman hovers anxiously, sponging Dorrie's forehead with tepid water. The girl struggles to stay calm. 'I can't stand this pain . . . please find something . . . anything.'

'I call a doctor for you. Redheads, you must watch . . . zey bleed like stuck pig, my mamma say,' Prin fusses.

'No doctor. This is our secret. Give me some brandy . . . pour some down my throat, quick!'

'I drink all ze brandy . . . I no sleep after you go. I 'av some pills. I go find them. Don't move!' A clatter down the stairs, the banging of cupboard doors as she rummages downstairs. 'Swallow these.' She spills the box of pills onto the bed and Dorrie gulps them down without a qualm. As she squirms, waiting for relief, Prin pads the sheets with towels and newspaper around the prostrate girl. Dorrie whimpers, struggling to her feet to pace around the room.

'Tell me something funny: a story, Prin, anything to take my mind off my body,' she pleads.

Renate Oblonsky sits herself down and strokes the girl's bony fingers. 'Once upon a time there was a pretty girl in Poland called Maria. She join ze ballet and travel all over the continent: to Rome, Paris and Vienna. Then she come to London and get sick just like you. She birth baby girl and they live in bad house in Billingsgate with nasty man who leave them alone every night. Each night she tell her little girl, you will be great dancer like me. She save pennies to find a teacher for her little princess. Then come day when she take daughter to the king of the ballet and he watch her dance. He thank ze mama and burst into laughter, at sight before him.

'"Why you bring zis creature to me? She av ze flattest feet and piano legs. She not know left hand from right. She tipple the chorus line like pack of cards. She'll go far but not in a tutu and point shoes. She too short, too klutz. Put her in the circus ring as a clown or the Music Hall, never in ze ballet!"

'So ze mamma go home and teach her how to sew fine seam, to stitch costumes, to darn ze point shoes. She say . . . don't listen to silly man. You, ma petite fleur, can be vat you vant. Choose any name, live your dreams and zey come true in your heart. To me you are my dancing daughter, now and forever!' The woman smiles mischievously.

'You old fraud, Renee White. So you're not even Polish!'

'Ah but I am, I was made on Polish soil by a Polish prince. Zat is enough for me. My name, I choose from a jeweller's shop in Whitechapel Road. I like the sound . . . Ob . . . Lonsky . . . This life; my best performance. It no rehearsal, Dorrie . . . so now you know, I tell only vous.'

By this time, Dorrie has her own show on the road, as she feels her pelvis split open and a ball of fire burning its way slowly, urgently into her groin . . . pushing, tearing deep inside. 'I need to pu . . . sh, I can't stop the pushing. What do I do?' she screams. 'I don't want a bloody baby.'

'Open ze legs . . . let me see. I have towels.' Prin pushes back the sheets, 'Yes . . . I see furry head. Quick big pushes, feather breaths, Prin is here to catch it.'

Dorrie strains, her eyes bulging with effort. The fireball moves in response. With one long scream, something slithers out, lying between the thighs, a girl child, bloody, bruise coloured and complete. Another gush and a lump of raw meat slides on the sheet. Not a sound. Dorrie takes one darting glance and knows no more.

When she wakens, the room is empty. Only the clock of St Mary's in the Market Square disturbs her stupor. It must be late but she is far too befuddled to count the chimes; out cold for hours in a dreamless sleep. Then she feels her flat stomach, remembers and turns for the child, but it is gone from her bed. Her head buzzes oddly. 'Prin . . . Prin where is it . . . the baby? Let me see her, bring her.' She calls out from her bed, neatly remade, with clean sheets and a wad of material between her legs. Prin stands by the door, her hands held in prayer, eyes down. 'Show me the baby, now.' The urgency of her plea forces a response.

'She no breathe. I not know vat to do. I take her away,' she simpers not looking Dorrie in the face.

'Where've you put her . . . you can't just take her away without me seeing her!'

'It best you no see baby, best . . . you have no place to take baby, Dorrie. She's at peace. No worry, I take care of it all for you.'

The girl tries to lift herself but the room swims around her and she flops back onto the pillow. 'I saw her. She was born alive, I'm sure. She must be buried, please for God's sake. I never wished her dead.'

'You better off wizout baby, nobody knows. Now you go away and start fresh over. Forget zis night.'

'I want my baby . . . I want her now. You haven't killed her, have you?' Dorrie screams, tears coursing down her cheeks. 'Don't do this to me . . . to your friend. Show her to me now.'

'You rest. I see vat I can do.' Prin slips out of the room, down the stairs out into the dark night. Dorrie rests fitfully, fighting sleep, waiting for her return.

She creeps through the foggy street, a faceless bundle in her arms, combing the back alleyways, the hedged and ancient windings of the city, for an entrance up to the Reservoir at Netherstowe. But the streets are not connecting into the familiar pattern. The moon hides in shame, giving no light to guide her on this terrible task. Her legs are heavy as lead, disobedient limbs slowing her progress. The windows of the sleeping city shuttered, blackened, closing ranks against her foul intent. Only three dark spires loom over her, watching, waiting. At last she finds the gap in the hedge; the gap well known to lovers, to the tow path, to hidden grassy ditches for secret trysts. There is no one in sight.

She stands by the edge of the water as it laps gently onto the cobblestones. No prayers can she mouth, only the pounding of her heart like a drumbeat before the guillotine. The bundle is launched, unprotected, defenceless into the water. She hears the plop, sees ripples circling. For a brief second there is a floating, then like a stricken vessel it tips, lurches and sinks out of sight. Suddenly her only concern is to reach out, to retrieve the parcel. She wades into the cold pool to save the drowning package but it has disappeared and she sinks with it beneath the surface, fighting for breath, panic pressing on her chest.

Dorrie wakes, tearing the sheets, wet with tears dripping down her face and milk leaking from her swollen breasts. Always the same haunting dream. 'I killed my baby, as sure as if I tied the cord around her neck. Why did I hate the idea of Lucky's child growing inside me? Why have I been so careless?' One glimpse of the plump tiny creature with fingers curled like fronds, the helplessness of her startled look, changes everything. The image flashes into her brain. The baby was not deformed but complete, pausing in shock between birth and life. How can she have not been breathing? Unless she suffered neglect, violated in the womb. I did not want her, so she was not born, the girl cries out. I do not deserve to be a mother so she is taken away from me.

For ten days she stays imprisoned in the attic, at the mercy of Prin's erratic nursing, force fed leftovers, sneaked from the café below. In the dining room her friends go about their business, unaware of her presence, unaware of her misery and shame. That must be part of her punishment. At night, when they have gone home, she roams the premises in a dirty kimono, black with garish dragons embroidered in silk, stinking of cigarettes and stale blood. She searches in every cupboard, suitcase, shoebox, investigates any bundle, bag, even outside in the garden, just in case, checking the soil for a newly dug grave. She peers down crannies with fixed intent, like a madwoman let loose in the night. She begs the Prin to show her the grave.

The old woman falls silent, averts her gaze. 'I do vat I think right. I do the best for you.'

'Well, you can stop all the phoney accent when you talk to me. I know your story. I don't believe you are telling me the truth. I think you killed her and buried her. Just show me where or I go to the police!' She waves her finger.

'Stop your threats! I do vat I think best. You just get strong. Go away from here, start again. Go to London. What is done is done. I can do no more now. I keep you safe, like you ask. I give you my rations. I tell no one, like you ask. That vat you want when you come to me. It all gone wrong. I know that now. Forget ze baby. Have many babies and you forget zis one. Brown babies, no one wants reminding . . . you will see.'

The small woman, her face tired, lifts her scissors to tailor a winter coat from an army blanket of tough grey wool.

'See, I make you fine coat out of Chad's blanket. He left me two whole ones.'

'I don't care if he left you a hundred. I'll not wear it. I wish I never came back here. I don't trust you anymore. I'll never trust you again. I thought you cared for me. Now I can't wait to get away from this cursed place!' Dorrie clatters up the wooden stairs, nursing her grievance with a bitter heart, and begins to pack.

Midnight

Dorrie was tired now, tired of tramping the stations of her cross. 'Tomorrow will be my dancing day.' She smiled as her head hit the pillow.

Once again she dreamt of a dancing child who skipped and twirled with waving arms and hair streaming, who coloured the dreams in an instant with a touch of her magic paintbrush, brightening the edges of her troubled sleep. Who was this creature with harlequin pants and scarlet ribbons? She often came to taunt and tantalise, so silent, always out of reach around the next corner? Tomorrow's child, tomorrow's hope perhaps . . .' The woman woke with a start. Only one more place to call. Tomorrow will take care of it.

Midnight

In her cottage, Isobel tossed and turned. Unfinished business, like an unpressed seam, was pulling the material of her life out of line. Invisible to the casual eye, it is to the seamstress a blemish, a distraction.

Unfinished business skulked in the shadows, stalking silently, reproachfully. 'Look at me . . . I'm still here to dog your heels.'

Unfinished business was the skeleton in the family cupboard, never unearthed; the earnest quest for an answer, too easily quenched in a wayside pub and forgotten.

Now, when there was time to chew the cud of life in peace, came faces at the window, waving for attention, sepia faces from crinkled photos too long exposed to light.

Tomorrow, Dorrie Goodman will call. Why should I stay and face the music, when pills are by my bed, waiting with the gift of sleep. There's enough in the bottle to launch myself out on that last journey into the lake of dreams.

I have to stay; there are others to consider. How I wish I could forget our last meeting in November 1944.

5

BELLE. SOLO

<u>Menu</u>

Winterwarming Soup

Steamed Fish Roll with Suet Crust Pastry and Chipped Potatoes

Mock Mincemeat Slice or Belle's Christmas Pud with Custard

November 1944

Belle Morton peers out into the street. Outside, lamplight twinkles cautiously since the lifting of some blackout restrictions, tempting Christmas shoppers to linger over their purchases with hot cups of Bovril before the bus journey home.

Wyn has gone home early, with 'one of her chests'. Belle feels unsettled, discovering that some of her pies have gone walkabout, as Digger would say! 'The flour fairy up to her old tricks, no doubt. I don't know where she puts the stuff,' she sighs, for Prin is as bony as a chicken carcass. Hard enough always being short staffed, without food going missing. 'One of these days I'll bake her a mustard pie and leave it in the cold store, with so much powder in it, she'll have to call out the fire brigade!'

Prin behaves oddly, peering over the banister, checking who is in or out. Yet sometimes when she does leave her rooms to shop or fit costumes, Belle could swear she can hear footsteps creaking on the floorboards overhead. But she knows it must just be her imagination working overtime. An odd piece of pie she tolerates now and then but someone has definitely been rooting in the cupboards, disturbing her supplies, crockery and pans shifted enough to arouse suspicion.

Now it is hard to raise enthusiasm for Christmas puddings, after six long years of war. Wyn still misses her friend Dorrie Goodman's company. Not a word from the minx in six months. Replacements come and go, hardly time to train them up before off they pop into the forces or better paid factory jobs. Sometimes when they're short, Maggie Preece will do a few hours or the Prin too: definitely a last resort. She wolfs down any scraps before they reach the kitchen door.

Autumn brought the best news through the letter box. A Red Cross postcard from Digger Carstairs, landing on the mat, telling them he was a guest of the Germans: only a temporary guest, she hopes, if newspaper optimism is to be believed.

The spirit of the Vic is stumbling at the last hurdle; tired, bored by the sameness of the course. Ideas bubble in Belle's stewpot, simmering away on the back burner for future reference. There is talk in the trade of a growing need for milk bars, places for young people to gather and have fun; all the rage in the United States; cookery books to write, for new wives setting up home after their demob, new ingredients to try, new techniques and new equipment to demonstrate. She must keep slogging on, rallying the troops, holding onto the regular custom. The old fire of challenge has gone, replaced by an aching loneliness, a hunger to put her arms around someone of her own.

It sounds as if a herd of elephants thunders above the ceiling, disturbing her train of thought, 'That's it, my girl! Sort out that damn woman once and for all,' she yells, racing up the stairs at the double, flinging open the living room door, to give the Prin a piece of her mind.

There in the middle of the floor kneels Dorrie Goodman, on the rag rug, packing a kitbag. One look at the girl and Belle stares shocked. Gone is the pretty full-faced schoolgirl, the statuesque figure, those luminous dark eyes, once so innocent and sparkling. Before her cowers a gaunt young woman in a shabby gaberdine mackintosh, her hair lank, dulled, scraped back in a bun, her face pale, drawn with dark half moons under her eyes; a shadowy ghost of her former self. 'Dorrie . . . my dear! What are you doing here?'

'I've been staying a while . . . I hope you don't mind,' she whispers, startled by the welcoming smile.

'Why didn't you come downstairs to see us all? Have we offended you?'

'Nothing like that, Mrs Morton . . . it's just that I've had a bad time recently. I need a bit of quiet. Prin understands me. I'm leaving now though, off to London on the train.'

'Are you still in the Land Army, then? Your mother pops in to see if we've heard from you. She's not looked well for a long time. We didn't know where you were.'

'I know . . . I had my reasons. I'll send you an address when I'm settled. I'm going to join up properly, in the A.T.S. or something . . . see the world and all that . . . while I have a chance. I need to get away.'

'Have you enough money, Dorrie? London is an expensive place.'

'I'll not starve.'

'You look as if you have been doing. Look at you . . . like a drink of water . . . so thin. Come on, tell me what's been the matter?'

'It's a long story, I haven't time. Ask the Prin, she knows all about it. Tell her she can explain everything,' mumbles the girl as she bounces the heavy kitbag down the stairs.

'I hope you've packed all your music,' Belle adds.

'It's all in there, a bit battered. It's about time it got an airing. Don't worry.'

'You will keep in touch? Promise! Wyn will be sorry not to see you. She's writing to your brother at sea . . . very regularly so she tells me.'

'Good, I'm glad. Sol deserves a nice girl like her.'

'Dorrie Goodman, something awful has happened, hasn't it? Tell me, I might be able to help.' Belle dives into the cash register and pulls out a handful of notes, shoving them into the girl's hand.

Dorrie draws back, shaking her head. 'I can't.'

'You will, my girl. Think of all the times you stopped me from bashing Connie Spear over the head with a saucepan! Remember Victory Pie and Chad. How we danced with those Yankee boys. They were good times, weren't they?'

'I suppose so,' nods the girl, close to tears.

'You take that money. You earned it and I can see you need it. Please let us know when you're famous and singing on the wireless. You will be, teacups or not!' Belle reaches out to give her a big hug. 'Mistakes can always be mended, Dorrie. Remember . . . she who never made a mistake, never made anything. I should know.' Belle laughs.

'No, Mrs Morton. There is no righting this wrong, believe me. Thanks for everything!' Dorrie shouts, as she flings open the door, disappearing across the Square into the gathering gloom.

Belle waits in her café, cleaning, polishing, tidying nervously, until she hears the turn of the lock and Prin's arrival from the fitting appointment in the Close. 'Right, Madame Oblonsky. Just what has been going on upstairs? Who has been ravishing my tins and raiding my pantry again? I want a proper explanation. No feeble excuses this time. I've already had one strange version from the secret lodger upstairs. Oh yes . . . I know who she is! So you needn't lie to me on her account.'

Prin drops the sewing case, as she collapses on the bottom of the stairs like an empty sack. 'Oh, Meez Morton. I do terrible thing. I don't know vat to do. Pleez you gotta help me. I vant tell you. She no let me.'

'Dorrie says you can spill the beans. Come on, let's have a brew and sort it out right now.'

'Oh, Meez Morton. I no mean harm, I know not vat is best for Dorrie. She like daughter to me. I so glad she came to me at first.'

'When was that then?'

'Two . . . three weeks ago . . . I lose track of time. I so upside down. I wan to tell you. Now you cross with poor refugee.'

'Come on, stop talking in riddles. Spit it out.' Belle leans over the table.

'She come to me . . . very big with Lucky's baby. She had to leave farm. Nowhere else to go. She very scared, no want brown baby, I think. I help her birth baby upstairs.'

'In the attic, that dirty place?'

'It not so bad, better than in some bus station. She has baby girl. I know not vat do. She fell asleep. I see to baby bits. I clean it up and I take it away.'

'You what?' gasps Belle.

'I took it away, little girl, very beautiful, very brown. I know she not want brown baby so, I wrap it in a towel and a copy of the *Daily Mail* and army blanket from Chad. I make ze other into smart coat for Dorrie but she no want.'

'But the baby, was it all right?'

'Perfect. I wrap it careful, it cold night and I put it in basket like Moses. I carry it down to the Minster pool path across the Post Office by the Park Gardens. I put it careful in telephone kiosk, safe and warm. People always phoning there. She warm as toast but she crying bit. I had to be back to check on Dorrie, in case she bleed. Redheads always bleed after birthing, my mamma say.'

'Oh Prin! What have you done?' Belle's heart thumps.

'Oh, Meez Morton, zat not all . . . when she wake, she cry out for baby so much. I tell her it no breathe. It dead and I take it to the priest to baptize . . . so it go to heaven. I tell big stories. She no believe me. She very angry, crying for her baby. So I go back again in dead of night. I put on my cloak and scarf, hide my face and creep out as fast as I can to the basket. But it gone, Meez Morton. All gone! . . . I don't know vat to do, I walk all streets, just in case. I no go police. They think I am drunk wiz such a story. I no shame my friend. So I think it for best she have no baby and go back. I can't tell her vat I do, so I say nothing. I do terrible think but I do for Dorrie so she go away wiz out burden, have new life.'

'You should have confided in me. I would never betray Dorrie. But you stole her child from her. You had no right.'

'I tell her now then. I make it right? You come viz me and we tell her?'

With sinking heart and trembling legs, Belle replies, 'But you can't tell her, you fool. She's gone!'

'Gone out?'

'No. She left for the London train, hours ago. I caught her packing when I heard a noise. I gave her money, sent her on her way. Oh God! Poor girl what have we both done?'

'But she never say goodbye to her Prin.'

'Do you blame her?'

'We find her, we write to her?' the old woman suggests, her hands shaking as she puffs a rollup.

'I have a feeling that Dorrie is not going to be so easy to find. People disappear in wartime. All we can hope for is that she keeps her promise.'

'Vat promise?'

'To keep in touch!' Belle crosses her fingers.

'Digger Carstairs, where are you when I need you? Your letters are only postcards.' Belle pats powder on her nose, tilts her best felt hat to a precarious perch, passes the strap under the plump roll of hair and inspects the effect with a sniff at her reflection. 'You're on your own with this one, chum!' She jabs in a hat pin for good measure and wrapping a musquash jacket tightly over her chest against the December chill, dawdles across the City to the police station with leaden feet.

At the sight of the blue lamp, she pauses for a deep gulp of air. Knocking at the enquiry window, Belle jumps as the moustached, fiery face of Constable Joby Goodman peers out at her in surprise. 'What can we do for you, Mrs Morton? . . . That blighter upstairs been stealing your rations again?'

'I have an appointment with the Inspector, for ten o'clock.'

The policeman searches the desk officiously. 'It's not down here. I shall have to see, he's a very busy man. Can I deal with the matter?'

'Thank you, Constable, but only the Inspector will do. We have spoken on the phone.' Belle smiles, trying to control her trembling. Why, oh why, would *he* of all Bobbies be on duty this morning? Her instincts are to turn tail and run but, as if on cue, a side door opens and the Inspector waves her through politely, barking to Goodman, 'Fetch the lady some tea and knock before you come in! Right, Mrs Morton . . . Isobel. We met at the Carol Concert at the Baverstocks . . . lovely house. Shame it's so full of refugees . . . Amazing woman, Belinda. Salt of the earth.' Belle shuffles in her chair. 'Forgive me, you didn't come for small talk. How can I be of assistance? It all sounded most mysterious on the phone.'

185

Belle clears her throat. 'Can I speak to you confidentially
. . . off the record?'

'That depends,' he advises, putting his hands together
into a pyramid, resting his elbows on the desk, intrigued.
'Carry on, please.'

'Just supposing a young girl gets herself into trouble, you
know how it is these days . . . and gives birth secretly,' her
voice descends to a whisper.

'Yes . . . go on,' urges the officer impatiently.

'Just supposing a misguided but well-meaning onlooker is
so concerned for her welfare that she removes said baby and
places it safely but, publicly where it will be found . . . in a
Moses in the bulrushes fashion.' Belle falters and the man
leans forward.

'Yes. Yes.'

'Just supposing that well-meaning but misguided friend
realises she made a terrible mistake and goes back to retrieve
the said basket, only to find it has vanished from the hidey
hole . . . I am here to ask you what might happen to the
baby and to such a misguided friend who put it there?'

The silence is ominous. The officer rearranges himself,
folding his arms. 'Was the alleged mother aware of the
intentions of her supposed friend?'

'No, not at all. She was told the baby was dead, so left the
city for the South, unaware of its existence and deeply
distressed.'

'I see. Was there anything else you might like to add to help in this enquiry – date, sex, that sort of thing?'

'Only that it could be female and of a distinctive colouring. All this happened around the middle of November, I think.'

Another silence. 'Well, Mrs Morton, just supposing all you have told me were to have occurred, I'm afraid that misguided friend, whoever she is, could be charged either under the 1861 Offences Against The Person Act or the Children and Young Persons Act of 1933. You can't just abandon a child as you please.'

'Inspector. This is not my doing. I am trying to repair the damage as best I can. Where might the baby be now?'

'Why do you want to know?'

'Because I could have prevented it all if I had followed my instincts and pushed a bit harder. I can't have a child put in an orphanage as a foundling, when I know that one parent is alive but unaware. Can I?'

'Can't you? It seems a perfectly logical place for, as you say, a distinctive child, handicapped by colour.'

'If we can trace her mother, surely the child's place is by her side?'

Joby Goodman hovers at the open door and places the cups down slowly, trying to catch the drift of this serious debate.

'That'll be all, Constable,' dismisses the officer with grim face. Belle rattles the cup on the saucer. The Inspector frowns. 'I think a crime has been committed and you are withholding evidence, my dear . . . an accessory after the fact.'

'I've told you everything I know.'

'Everything, except the name of the mother. I have to have that name before we can proceed further in this matter. I must have the name, please.'

Belle mouths the name silently.

'Good God! Does he know?'

'No, sir, and he must not, I beg you. She left home many months ago. It is none of their business. I am hoping she will contact me. She promised to keep in touch. Can you imagine anyone wanting this made public?'

The Inspector wipes his glasses on a handkerchief and mops his brow. 'Well! Of all people! It would kill him . . . such a proud man, refused promotion for years. Says his reward in Heaven is sufficient. Dedicated chap is Goodman but I can't see him as the doting grandfather to a tar baby! Leave it with me. I'll set the ball rolling down the hill, but I'm not promising any mercy for that friend of yours. It may all be too late.'

Leaving the station, Belle is in no mood to return to her work but scurries with sinking heart through the streets, back to her rooms. 'What have I done? Where will this all end?'

December 1944

The summons from the Inspector comes three days before Christmas, right in the middle of Mollie Custer's annual Christmas bun fight for the Dainty Dots. Wyn and the Prin are left to hold the fort, against the jelly and custard high spirits splattering the walls of the Vic.

Belle rattles and jerks out of the city in Bindy Baverstock's Austin Seven, borrowed for the occasion, clanking the gears, double declutching nervously. It is a long time since she was at the wheel of a car. Mona, her Morris Eight had been sold long ago, to finance the café. She crosses the Stafford Road into Abnall's Lane, a winding narrow country road, rising steeply from the city, passing the gracious gatehouses. She marvels at the gorge with its layers of rusty pink earth revealing slabs of sandstone etched with grey lichens and emerald green moss. The gorge arches over with holly and evergreens against a cobalt sky. Belle stalls the engine, pausing to admire the open view, then chugs on towards the Military Hospital and the Asylum, with its bleak gothic turret. She heads northwards, up narrow lanes, in the direction of the ancient hunting forest of Cannock Chase.

The Cottage Homes are a cluster of neat red brick houses, set in spacious gardens that now sprout vegetables, tended by boys who hoe and fork over the soil. The Homes are loosely attached to a grim fortress of a workhouse. A few paper chains cannot disguise institutional chilliness. Belle shivers at the thought of so many innocent lives stranded in this place. As she strolls down long corridors, with dark green painted walls and treacle paintwork, she sniffs a school dinner smell of boiled cabbage and disinfectant.

This is a loveless place for babies: clean and efficient, but no home for Dorrie's child. The matron, in dark uniform and starched head-dress, summons Belle swiftly to her office.

'I gather you have come to select an infant from the Nursery, Mrs Morton. You will have to fill in all the forms and see the Welfare.'

'Not select, just collect on a temporary basis, for a friend.'

'This is not a Sorting Office, you know ... Which offspring might that be?' Belle explains the story briefly.

'You mean the bus stop baby?'

'No, the one in a telephone box.'

'Oh that one!' The matron peers at her closely. 'You know the mother then? Don't know what the world is coming to! So many half castes. No colour bar with our silly girls, is there? The flood of D-Day babies we are placing. Come with me,' says Matron stiffly. 'I want to show you something.'

Belle marches down another corridor, through a labyrinth of turnings and twistings to a huge nursery full of canvas cots. The noise is deafening; a room full of crying babies, snuffling little grunting creatures, tightly swaddled in blankets, red faced and yelling with fury, while the nurses go about their duties unperturbed.

'We let them cry. It is good for their lungs and we haven't time to spoil them with unnecessary handling.' Belle is still reeling from the din and the smell. 'Look around you, my dear, we are inundated with D-Day babies, little souvenirs no one wants to keep. The aftermath of too many Yanks and some very silly girls with not enough to do but chase after anything in trousers.' Matron parades up the aisle of cots and pauses. 'Fortunately there's a steady demand for the fair haired, blue eyed variety of course: nice little English babies are easy to place. The Colonies are crying out for children and some will be shipped out as soon as the war is over.' She beckons her over to the far end of the room and points to a row of cots, full of dark-skinned babies with black eyes and thick lashes. 'This lot are never going to be placed are they? The tar babies we call them . . . poor mites. A row of brown babies no one wants to own up to. We keep them together.'

Belle leans anxiously over each cot. The matron dismisses her charges. 'Oh they are poppets now . . . but just imagine in a few years' time how they will stick out! The older girls call them their chocolate babies and wheel them out for fresh air.'

'Which is the telephone baby?'

'Are you sure you wouldn't prefer the one from the bus stop? It's almost white.'

'Quite sure, thank you. Which one am I looking for?' Belle searches each cot, then pauses at the last cot with a pink label attached. The infant, eyes open, stares at the flickering of her approach: a baby with frizzled brown hair and coffee coloured skin.

'You've spotted her then, our little Olive. Suits the name. Quite a cutie, but as I said, they are as babies. We keep them strictly to a Truby King routine, no picking up and spoiling. We are very short of staff so they have to be left to amuse themselves.'

'Can I hold her?' Belle asks, tentatively unwrapping the swaddling blanket, lifting her up, feeling the dampness of her nightdress. 'She's soaking.'

'They all are by this time. We deal with that later, dear.'

She means well, thinks the visitor sadly, as she stares into the dark eyes so old and world weary, blinking back at the attention. 'This is no place for you, not for such a smasher. Look at your lovely long legs, just like Lucky's lamp posts.

Fancy calling you Olive. You need a tall name, a happy name . . . come on, let's get your supplies. You are not stopping here when there are willing hands and doting aunties to mind you until your mum comes marching home. I know it's madness. I don't know where we'll put you. What I know about baby care can be written on my hat pin but I can soon learn.' Belle prattles and chirrups as she bumps them both down to Lichfield, back to the Cathedral spires, those Three Ladies of the Vale, standing tall and proud in the valley, awaiting their return.

Sunday Morning

Isobel prowled through the cottage at dawn searching for some peace. She made herself a strong cup of tea.

They were all curious. Prin knew of course, the Preeces wondered and Bindy guessed. No one dared to tackle my decision or face my stubbornness. Look what the doctor brought in his bag, I laughed, as they peered into the bassinet with astonishment. Someone had to look after these little mites, the orphans of war, I told my customers. I was only doing my duty . . . Who am I fooling, silly old biddy!

It was love at first sight; when I sniffed her head and she nuzzled into my heart, through all the layers of my good intentions.

Sunday Morning

Dorrie ate a hearty breakfast, bacon and eggs, toast and a pot of strong black coffee. She wiped her lips with satisfaction on a crisp linen napkin, her belly barrel-full.

It was right to come back, to check out the old place. I have nothing to fear from it now. No one recognised me. Why should they? I am just another wrinkled face. The old are invisible if they are not eccentric. Perhaps thirty years ago I would have turned a few heads.

Not all my life was pain and anguish. The golden moments came when I buried my secret in a kitbag, dumped it on Euston Station and re-invented myself.

6
CASSIE

<u>Menu</u>

Pea and Ham Broth

Spam Fritters with Vegetables or Farmhouse Cottage Pie

Jam Roly Poly Pudding or Railway Slice with Custard

January 1945

'Next!' barks the disembodied voice from the orchestral stalls to a queue of hopefuls, trembling in the wings for an audition.

'When the red red robin comes bob, bob, bobbin along . . .' warbles a would-be Shirley Temple, out of tune.

'Next!'

'This is my lovely day,' launches forth a soprano, built like an ocean liner.

'Next!'

Dorrie stumbles into the spotlight, trying to look as if she ate auditions for breakfast, praying her smart new slacks and lamé crossover shirt, her hair caught in a sophisticated golden net snood will cover her terror. 'Bless this house, oh Lord, I pray, Keep it safe by night and day . . .' she pauses, waiting for her dismissal.

'Carry on,' comes the order and she sings through her repertoire.

'Name?'

'Cassie Gordon.'

'And where have you been hiding yourself, then?'

'Singing for evangelists, Gospel choirs . . . and a G.I. Band,' the lies roll from her mouth like polished pebbles. Dorrie holds her breath. 'Is this happening to me?'

Was it only three weeks since her forlorn arrival at Euston Station when, desperate to lose her past, she had resorted to the oldest of ploys: reporting her handbag, containing ration card and identity, stolen on the train. In that brisk walk from Police Station to Recruiting Office, she toyed with a wardrobe of new identities. God bless the sergeant at the Recruiting Office, who had believed every tearful word, given her a cup of tea and asked her what she did in civvy street.

'I'm a singer, but I don't suppose the Army can use my services?' she joked, blushing at this subterfuge.

'Just where you're wrong, young lady. Ever heard of E.N.S.A.?'

'Every, Night, Something, Awful!' she retorted, remembering the Airmen in the Victory Café, who moaned about the boring concert parties held in the Hangars.

'That's a bit unfair,' said the sergeant, but laughed all the same. 'They are always on the lookout for new talent. Get yourself down to Drury Lane Theatre and see if they can fix you up . . . good luck!'

So clutching a new name, age and identity and the last of Belle's money, she had scoured Oxford Street for clothes suitable for a rising star. 'This is the life for me!'

Two weeks later, as she bumps up a mountain path in a rackety charabanc on the way to her first engagement, she is not so sure. And that's after four hours on a sooty train, heading towards the remotest corner of the North Riding, hugging a battered suitcase full of second-hand hired evening gowns, smelling to high heaven, hastily altered to fit her new slim shape. Even her Leichner stage make-up is loaned, on pain of death, by a soft-hearted chorus girl. She sniffs her cleansing cream with relish, just to make sure this is not all a dream.

The other 'professionals' keep themselves to themselves, fussing for the best seats on the bus: an elderly tenor, who sports a suspicious rug of rabbit fur on his head; a concert pianist, with corkscrew curls and bosoms like the cones of bomber planes; a violinist with a sad lined face and smouldering latin eyes.

This is my first paid appearance in public, Dorrie smiles to herself. Never mind the torrential rain, the frosty company, the brief rehearsals or the venue in a converted cowshed, with the pong of manure still ripe in the air. Nothing dampens her spirit. The pianist may moan about the consumptive state of the piano. The violinist snaps his bow as he warms up. The strip of footlights has mysteriously disappeared and the shippon roof is leaking, but to Dorrie it might as well be the stage of Sadler's Wells, when she wobbles on the pallets, draped in carpet, belting out her numbers to a fidgety audience, drawn from nearby outposts for the show. There is a caterwauling of whistles and cries for More! Which does not seem to please the rest of the Starlight Troupe. Icicles twinkle backstage after the performance.

'Did I do all right?' she asks innocently.

'You'll do,' says the tenor, adjusting his toupee.

'Praise indeed,' sighs Dorrie in the farmhouse, as she tucks into steaming potato pie with a suet crust as thick as a doormat. Later she flops into a cupboard, on a bed as hard as a rock garden, curling herself into a ball. Only then does she weep, rocking her lost baby in her arms.

The routine is always the same. First the journey, then the rehearsal; a quick cup of stewed tea, spam fritters and a slab of army cake; a brief feet up and then a flip round the shops for some fresh air and privacy. The dressing room is often only a corner curtained off with a sheet; no decent lights to put on make-up. After the show comes sausage and mash in the mess and home to cold digs in the dark. Occasionally a 'big name' joins them for the evening, with a trunk of pressed costumes, a glamorous whiff of expensive perfume and tailoring and then a brisk no nonsense exit, for the top of the bill, to the nearest decent hotel or the officers' residence.

'This is my apprenticeship and I'll put up with anything to survive in this business' is the Mae West that keeps her spirits afloat, even in the roughest, most mundane of factory engagements. Her solo spots increase and she finds, now and then, she is allowed to finish off the first half of the Starlight Show.

Somewhere between Inverness and St Ives, Cassie Gordon transforms herself into Cassie Starlight, into Cassie Starr, singer with any showband that will give her good backing. Then comes the final accolade: an eight week tour overseas alongside chorus girls and acrobats. The destination is secret for the war drones on in Europe.

Sunday Morning

Dorrie smiled as she checked out her hemline in the mirror. Old habits die hard when appearance matters.

Be careful what you wish for, it may come true, they say. How was I to know, when I ditched poor Dorrie, that I would end up warming up troops for the star turn, singing in dingy barracks, riding on camel's back to sing for 'desert rats' on makeshift stages in the sand dunes!

Cassie Starr, my tinsel name, has seen me through the best of times, the fifties feasts, singing on Variety Bandbox and Workers' Playtime on the wireless, the Palladium shows, starring in pantomime in the best theatres, a Jaguar with personal number plates and my own mink coat. It didn't last, of course, not for me or David Whitfield, Josef Locke, Yana, Lita Rosa in the lean years of the sixties.

Where are we all now . . . Those faded faces on sixpenny sheet music, crackling on 78 records, sold for pennies in car boot sales; all of us blasted into orbit by television and the Mersey beat.

Never go back I told myself and I did not, except for one brief passing through, which hardly counts.

April 1964

Cassie Starr parks her Triumph Herald slap in the middle of Lichfield Market place and dashes to the red brick loo, tucked in the corner by the Corn Exchange. On her way north for the Summer season on Blackpool Pier, it is only a small detour off the A5 to give the place the once over.

The bus station has disappeared but the statue of Doctor Johnson still patrols the Square. Window boxes are sprouting bright daffodils despite the chill of a late spring. It is half-day closing and the pavements are empty. Her made-up eyes rove instinctively across the street to the old house. It is painted white with LA CASA BLANCA COFFEE BAR emblazoned in black letters above the window of what was once the Victory Café.

The chill easterly ruffles her fashionable bob, cuts through the leopardskin, fun fur jacket, pulling her towards the warmth of a tearoom. Only the smoky fug is still the same.

The walls are stuccoed in white plaster on which garish posters of bullfighters and toreadors pose and posture with arrogant calves. The ceiling is lowered with netting, in which dangle plastic crabs and sea shells. In the corners hang Spanish flags and lanterns. Each table has a tired dusty bottle of Mateus Rose, dripping with candle grease, a souvenir ashtray from Spain and a bowl of Demerara sugar. The coffee, brought to the table by a sullen young waitress with a pony tail, chewing gum, is slopped in a glass cup and plonked onto the table with the bill. The liquid is an apology for the real cappuccino served in the King's Road but Cassie is glad of its warmth. She stares around sadly. Not all change is progress. In the corner, under the stairs now boarded off, stands a majestic juke box, playing the latest on the Hit Parade. Not one name of the recording artists does she recognise. The café hums to the noisy debate of a group of earnest young men in duffle coats.

'How long has this been a coffee bar?' Cassie asks the waitress politely.

'Dunno,' answers the girl, staring at her. 'It were a milk bar when I was little.'

'Do you remember it as the Victory Café? Mrs Morton had it then,' Cassie adds, trying to look enthusiastic about the dishwater taste.

'Dunno, I'll ask in the back, if you like.' Cassie catches a glimpse of a dark Spanish-looking girl, peering out from the kitchen, who smiles at her interest. The waitress pauses for a moment. 'I've seen your face somewhere . . . are you off the telly? I won't be a moment.'

Cassie slurps the dregs for the lumpy sugary bits, leaves some coins for a tip and makes for the door.

Sunday Noon

Dorrie packed her overnight bag carefully, pausing to listen to the Cathedral bells as they peeled out across the city, such a tranquil overture to the day.

Never go back and here I am, waiting for the performance, waiting in the wings again with stage fright for the last act; a finale long overdue.

Isobel baked scones and her Yorkshire cheese tarts. She could do them blindfold and they never failed to impress. Her eyes darted to the kitchen clock, stomach churning like a cement mixer.

Why does she have to include me in her pilgimage of Grace? I hope she doesn't stay too long. Perhaps she has a bus to catch this evening. Then I can settle down to Songs of Praise or Coronation Street and rest in peace.

A carillon of bells carried away present thought, to drown in the flood from the past.

7

VE DAY

Menu

Bortsch
(our beetroot soup. God bless Russia!)

Victory Pie (a bean bake all the way from America)
or Roast Beef of Olde England with Yorkshire Puddings

Celebration Pudding
(a chocolate dream)

May 1945

Belle wakes early. 'So this is it, Victory in Europe!' The Cathedral bells, practising their rusty peals, ring out the long-awaited news. From early morning, Victory has been the word on everyone's lips. The city bustles with shoppers buying in bread to last out the two days' official celebrations.

Belle bakes from dawn to dusk; pies, pastry, trays of buns for street parties, while flags and bunting are draped from windows to lamp posts, to add to the festive mood. Every ounce of red white and blue cloth blazes out from the shop fronts. Union Jacks flutter from every flagpole. The pavements are hot with soldiers and airmen, their girls hanging on every available arm, snapping photos furiously at anything which moves. All trying to capture the moment for their future grandchildren. Wirelesses crackle loudly, as ears strain for the final announcement of peace.

The balmy May morning promises a lovely evening; perfect to stroll around the city and let off steam! In the public houses in Market Street, regulars hang around, waiting for news of extensions to drinking hours, school closures, for party time to begin. Searchlights are to be turned on the Cathedral face, flooding the building with golden light for the special Service of Thanksgiving to be held as part of the Victory celebrations. Lichfield is '*en fête*'.

Excitement in the Vic reaches fever pitch when a bunch of drunken airmen snake in and out of the café in a Conga, catching hold of Wyn and Belle, pulling them out into the street in a wild, jumping frenzy of yelling. Round the square they dance and holler to passers by, who join in the revels.

'It's all over, I can't believe it . . . Bindy Baverstock. All over,' yells Belle to her friend, who stands with her daughter, wistfully.

'Not quite,' she sighs, thinking of husband Simon, entombed in a Japanese POW camp in Singapore. 'What about the boys out east?'

'It can't be long . . . he'll come home and Digger will come home . . . one day soon, they'll all be home for good.'

'Not all.' Wyn pauses, out of breath. Her dad will not be coming home from Italy, nor Solomon Goodman from his resting place on the bed of the Atlantic. There will be many lost faces to remember and mourn.

Belle stops and touches her arm. 'I've not forgotten them, Wyn. But just for now . . . we all deserve a break . . . some time to let our hair down and take a breather.'

In the distance they can see the Prin pushing a pram, bedecked with bunting. Belle beckons her over and props up the baby, plumping the pillows behind her back. 'Let's have a photo of us all . . . the staff of the Victory Café. All us wonderful women who have filled thousands of empty bellies. Think of all those hot dinners we have served; all the belts we have loosened! We deserve a medal for unstinting service to mankind; civility in the face of non-stop moaning, complaints, shortages, rationing. Congratulations to you all!'

Then a giant soldier pulls her into the Square, into the revels in the street, into a dancing circle of children and shop girls. She finds herself captured by a ribbon of dancers, who whisk her up and then deposit her like flotsam on the pavement, gasping for breath. Belle lifts the baby high, to show her the scene but the infant only blinks sleepily. At six months, her golden limbs are plump, the white smocked romper suit already outgrown. 'Come on, Victy, it's bedtime for you, young lady.'

It was Sid Sperrin who had come up with a solution to her naming. 'She can't be, "the baby at the Vic" for ever, can she, Mrs Morton?' He stared solemnly at the woolly bundle in the borrowed blue pram. 'Why don't you call her Victy?'

'Why not?' She smiled to herself, knowing that no other café had a customer born on their premises, albeit in secret.

This naming, like Topsy, just grew and grew, from the humble Vic to Victorine, to the queenly Victoria, deemed too grandiose a handle for a baby. So they fell back on a comfortable, 'Victy'. Her arrival aroused intense curiosity and gossip at first. For once, the Prin was a soul of discretion and the secret held; Mrs Morton was known only as one of the kindly band of informal foster mothers 'doing her bit for the Community'.

The landlady refused to condone a child in her rooms, throwing Belle into a flurry of house hunting. It was fortunate that a friend of Bindy, in the Close, offered to rent her a small terraced house in Gaia Lane, at the back of the Cathedral moat. Most days, Victy spent her time in the garden of the café when the weather was fair, or upstairs with her devoted slave and nursemaid, Prin, in her rooms, if it was not. At first, it was only a temporary arrangement but as weeks have passed into months, hope of ever locating Dorrie Goodman has long faded.

They troop back into the dining room to survey the party wreckage of bunting, streamers and fizzy pop bottles with a sigh. Belle takes a deep breath and begins the clearing up, while Wyn sweeps the floor and collects the rubbish in a flour sack. Suddenly she stops. 'I know that handwriting. Where did this postcard come from? Must have slipped under the rug or got kicked out of sight in the dancing.

Look see ... if that's not Dorrie's handwriting, I'm a chinaman.' Holding Victy on her hip, Belle hunts for her glasses, while the Prin screams out.

'A camel in ze desert; look Meez Morton she let us know.' She waves the exotic scene in front of everyone's nose. 'Vat it say ... queek!' The writing is squeezed into every corner; the postmark indecipherable.

DEAR ALL. Just a line to say, all's well that ends well. I am singing for the troops (where sand gets up your nose). Tune into Forces radio, folks, and you might hear you-know-who some day soon. Tell Prin she was right. If you drop me a line, make sure you direct it to E.N.S.A. Moving on soon. Love Dorrie.

Belle re-reads the words slowly and silently. In the kitchen, Prin is burping the baby over her shoulder, jiggling her with excitement. 'Mamma come soon, little princess. We write to her now, long letter. Isn't she going to have a big surprise? Vunderbar! I think I cry, Meez Morton.'

'Whatever for?' snaps Belle, her cheeks flushed with irritation as she wipes out the last of the chocolate pudding with her finger.

'Peace in Europe, for my poor Poland and card from Dorrie; all in one day. All you need now, is for Diggerman to walk in door ... Vunderbar.'

'I suppose so,' was the flat reply.

'You look as if you lost bob and find tanner. Let's find another bottle in cellar and get ourself lit up!'

Belle folds the terry nappies carefully from the washing line, tucks the quilt tightly around the sleeping baby. She surveys the podgy cheeks, snub nose and curling eyelashes, soft and smooth, mahogany against the white satin pillow. A nest of rats gnaws within her stomach, biting deep into her gut. The Prin uncorks a dusty bottle.

'We write to Dorrie straight way. She forgive me when she see her Victy?'

'Hang on, Prin, don't rush, this is a delicate matter. You just can't spring a baby on a girl if she's out in the Middle East on tour. They won't fly her home. She can't drop her obligations. She needs to be told slowly, gently. Think what you did to her. Don't rush it.'

'Yes . . . I see, but we let her know, we get her postcard . . . Yes?'

'Yes, of course, I'll see to that next week. After all, only you and I know the whole story, remember? Everyone thinks I'm fostering an orphan child. We mustn't spill any beans. It's not fair to Dorrie, not until she comes to claim her. There are no names on her birth certificate. Victy is a foundling. You must be discreet, if ever it came to light that you abandoned her in a kiosk . . . well who knows how the police may react? You could be sent to prison . . . who knows?' Belle winces at her own words, watching the look of terror in Prin's eyes; her mouth gaping to reply, suddenly silent.

'How do we know Dorrie will believe our story?'

She picks the postcard from Prin's frozen fingers and pops it quickly into her pocket. The Prin, limp and weary, drags herself up the stairs without another word. One by one, Belle watches her layers of justice, fairness and sympathy peel away, like unwanted clothes in a heatwave, revealing the savagery of her true feelings.

She is my child now, not yours. Victy is mine. I named her, cuddled her colic, nursed her fears. I am the face she smiles at, my lips are the ones she mimics. It is me she watches with those black intense eyes from the pram I drove twenty miles to find. We must not disrupt her life yet. A few more months will make no difference. Dorrie needs time to adjust. We need time to adjust too. Dorrie will have to make a career for herself before they will hand her over. How can she cope with a baby in a trunk? No hurry with this affair . . . Fear stalks Belle. She will vet the post every day. As for this card, smiling, she ignites the gas ring and torches it in the frying pan.

'Have you heard anything?' begs the Prin.

'Not a word . . . give it time.'

'But it's three months since she wrote to us. I will write to E.N.S.A. myself. Give me ze address.'

'You give me your letter and I'll pop it in with my own.'
One by one the letters go up in smoke.

'She has her career to think about now. The past is best
forgotten.'

'Perhaps she no get our letter?'

'Perhaps not. Be patient,' says Belle, her skin growing
tough, taut, tightening like a drumskin, with each lie.

Victy cannot cope with change now, she is just learning
to stand and stagger around the furniture, biting her teeth on
any surface, dribbling with excitement. My child is so beautiful; all I ever wanted from life. All I shall ever have now. I
will not share my Victy. It is too late. I have to think of her
future now.

September 1945

The garrisons empty their conscripts in ill-fitting demob suits onto the Lichfield streets. The markets bulge with army surplus bargains. Wyn Preece and the Prin forget to check the post and listen avidly now to the Forces network on the wireless, waiting for Dorrie's promised debut.

Belle can begin to relax her working schedule to fit Victy's naps and playtime, preferring to wheel her around Beacon Park, to feed the ducks by Minster pool and join other younger mothers at the Welfare clinic. At first they glance slyly sideways at the obvious discrepancy between this mother and baby. Belle ignores their curiosity, fussing over their offspring, discussing baby matters like a veteran, until they begin to accept her as one of the regulars.

'Husband in the Forces still?' a woman asks, eyeing her left hand. Belle nods, grateful for the thin gold band and her married title without which this fostering would never have been considered.

Where on earth was poor old Dennis now? The thought of once being one of the Morton clan seems like a long forgotten dream. Neither had served divorce papers on the other and this suited her plans well.

As she saunters back to the café, the September leaves are curling, ready to drop with the first frost, the air tinged with woodsmoke. The streets are more peaceful; the city swopping military uniform for the comfortable old tweeds of a country market town. The same old faces in the café, smiling at the baby, the same tired menus and faithful staff. Suddenly Belle's spirit is sunk by the sameness of it all. She pops Victy in the playpen and turns to the same old tasks: making lists, checking supplies, replacing the Izal tissues in the toilet. Feeling every one of her thirty-eight years, she inspects the dusting of silver hairs at her temples. 'Fair, fat and nearly forty, my girl! Not a pretty sight!'

Suddenly a cap whistles past her ears and a coil of blue cigar smoke wafts into view. 'Look what the wind's blown in, my bewt!' She spins around towards the voice. There stands Digger, a scrawny sight, lines on his face like furrows in a ploughed field. Belle flings her arms around him with a scream. Now the picture is complete. The final piece of her jigsaw is at hand.

'Heavens! You've come back. How wonderful. What was it like being a guest of Jerry's? And I must look such a mess. I haven't put my face on.'

'You look just the same . . . lovely. How I've remembered you all. Used to sit on my bunk and eat five helpings of your apple pie in my head . . . Didn't think much of Jerry's hospitality but we got our own back, I can tell you!'

'I can't believe this. We thought you were back in Australia by now.' Digger follows her into the kitchen slowly, closing the door behind him, gathering her into his arms, to kiss her mouth and send her senses reeling at his touch. 'Oh Digger . . . it's been so long and I've missed you. So much to tell you. Wait till I tell the girls. Prin is out,' Belle adds.

'Still stuck with the old fraud? You're too soft hearted.' He nuzzles her nose.

'Fancy you rolling up like a bad penny! Thin as a beanpole. We'll soon get some flesh on those cheeks! What made you come back?'

'As if you need ask! For a slice of Victory pie and a proposition, Belle Morton.' Belle stirs her precious sugar ration into his tea cup in a daze.

'Steady on, love, with that sugar. How do you fancy opening up down under? Home cooking for the Pommy hordes, who will surely be on their way now this show is over?' Digger laughs into her eyes, hugging her again.

223

Belle sits down opposite him. 'Room for a little one too?'

'Anyone you like, love,' he twinkles.

'No, seriously, I mean a little one . . .' She smiles, pointing to the playpen in the outhouse, where Victy stands, curious, throwing her rag dolly across the flagstone floor.

'Who the hell is that?'

'Victoria, Victy, my little girl.' Belle smiles proudly.

'Like hell she is . . . she's a bleedin' Abo . . .'

'Don't say that . . . she is my foster child . . . she was abandoned.'

'Not surprised . . . that colour.' The furrows on his brow deepen into ditches, his mouth sneers into a hard line.

'Oh, Digger, look at her, she's beautiful and sharp as lemon drops. She wants you to play with her. Pick her up, she won't bite you.'

'No, love, she may be lovely to you but where I come from, she ain't goin' ter fit in, not that shade. Hell! Woman, you know how to spring it on a bloke! Never wrote a word about this little sprog. You can't just dob this one on me. She must be a year old.' Digger rises from the chair and backs towards the door.

'Not quite. Surely you don't expect me to leave her behind, dump her in some orphanage?'

'Why not, if that's where you really found her?'

'What do you mean? Are you suggesting that I am lying to you?'

'It wouldn't be the first time a guy's been saddled with someone else's kid. Let's be honest . . . when men are away, women still play!'

'Get out! Bugger off to your land of milk and honey, sunshine and canned fruit . . . if you think for one minute . . .' Belle plonks the baby onto her hip. 'Don't say another word, Digby Carstairs. Where I go, she goes from now on. She's the only good thing to come out of this war!'

'Suit yerself. I'm sorry, Belle. You should have given me some warning.' Digger lifts his cap from the floor. 'I'll leave you to it then! If you change your mind . . .'

Belle shakes her head weakly, her legs trembling, as he retreats through the open door. 'I want to go with you.'

'I'm sorry,' he mutters as he closes the door.

'So am I.' Belle weeps, for it is too late now, to tell the truth.

Later, as she clears away the debris of toys from the kitchen floor, she hears the Prin singing a Polish lullaby to the fractious child on her lap. The tune floats from room to room, a sad haunting air in the minor key, echoing her own mood, soothing its heaviness. She wipes a tear from the end of her nose and sniffs, listening to the Prin prattle into the wide eyes of the baby, who is fighting sleep. 'Your mamma is a beautiful Princess who meets a handsome soldier at a ball but they cannot be together. She sing to you one day on the wireless and come to fetch you home.'

'Stop that! At once!'

'But it true. I tell her about her mamma.'

'The past is past, I forbid you to fill her head with such nonsense. It will only unsettle her.'

'But it not right that you keep her to you. You do not try to find her mamma. I no think you ever look for Dorrie anymore. So I will go to policemen and tell them myself vat I do!'

Belle snatches the baby and smoothes down her nightdress. 'Do you think they will believe a crazy old woman . . . I shall deny it all,' she bluffs. 'And if they do, we will both be charged with perjury. What will happen to Victy then? Do you think Constable Goodman would take her in?'

'I no understand you. You send off poor Diggerman, with the fleas in his ears, as you say. I think you wicked woman. You do wrong for Dorrie.' The nursemaid throws down the bib on the table.

'Well if that is how you feel, you know what to do then. The war is over. It's about time, Renee White, you found yourself another billet. I have my own plans for the upstairs.'

Sunday Afternoon

Isobel swept through her cottage like a dervish, dusting, watching the clock with thudding heart. Then the thought of the coming encounter overwhelmed her and she sank in a chair to calm the palpitations.

'Steady the Buffs, old girl, stop all this nonsense! You did your best for all concerned. You saw them all off, one by one. Digger let me down. He had to go. Prin interfered once too often and got her marching orders. Bindy Baverstock disapproved so I distanced myself. None of them understood my position. Dorrie stayed away too long.

The fibres of love bound Victy and me tightly together. How could I cut her free? Not even King Solomon with all his wisdom would judge against me, after she was three, four, five. You can't take a child from its mother.

Each precious year sealed her as my own, I strewed her path with every opportunity, ballet lessons and music tuition, tennis coaching and elocution. Victy was a model child, secure in my devotion. Children are our future. She deserved the best and she never let me down.

Possession is, after all, nine tenths of the law. Adoption papers saw to that. Finders keepers; losers weepers. Tough, but that's life.

8

REPRISE

<u>*Afternoon Tea*</u>

Stilton and Walnut Flan

A Selection of tasty Sandwiches

Golden Scones with Jam and Cream

Yorkshire Cheese Tarts

Chocolate Yoghurt Cake

Earl Grey or Assam Tea

November 1994

At three o'clock, Dorrie left the hotel clutching her bags, head bending into the wind whipping across Stowe Pool. She paused by the Dr Samuel Johnson's willow on the gravel path and looked towards the back of the Cathedral.

A small dinghy bobbed on the pool, its sails dipping with the force of the wind. On the tow path, family groups paraded their tricycles and dogs. The city was geared to leisure now, not war; parks and playing fields, festivals and funfairs. Even the Cathedral Close was spruced up and floodlit for the tourists. As always, one of the three spires was encircled in scaffolding. At the West door, she stopped to admire the tiers of carved statues rising majestically up the wall. The piazza thronged with the Evensong congregation.

Vicar's Close, her final destination, set back from the Cathedral Close through an archway, was a hidden alleyway of medieval cottages, a winding line of higgledy piggledy buildings, huddled together like drunks for support. Already lamps were lit in the mullioned windows, as the residents settled themselves in for the evening, sipping tea or playing bridge around small tables. She tapped the knocker and waited, as a tabby cat curled itself round her ankles, grateful to be let in from the chill. The door opened cautiously, a pinched face smiled briefly.

'Oh it is you then, Dorrie Goodman. Come in, come in . . . I wouldn't have recognised you from Adam. You've put on some weight . . . come in, it's sharp out there! And you've gone all white . . . but then redheads often do.'

'You've shrunk to nothing, Belle Morton,' said the visitor as she entered the cottage with honey beamed ceilings. A log crackled on the fire. The sitting room was cluttered: an oak dresser crammed with plates and antique coffee cups, the sofa draped with a cotton patchwork quilt, a faded oriental carpet square over the parquet floor. The welcome smell of baking wafted through from the kitchen. 'Do I detect some scones in the air? You always were the Scone Queen. I can never get mine to rise.'

'I'll give you my recipe if you like,' replied the hostess eagerly as she carried her trophies, golden, crusted, to the coffee table. 'It was a surprise to get your note, right out of the blue. How did you know where to find me?' She poured the tea from a silver pot, with shaking hands.

'Everyone knows Baking Belle. You're quite a Burgess of the City now; a cottage in the Close, a seat on the Bench; a pew in the Cathedral and Chair of so many committees, I heard.'

'That's what comes of staying too long in one place, I suppose. You get nailed into the fabric after a while.' Belle brushed the crumbs from her pleated varuna wool skirt, touching the string of pearls that shimmered in the firelight, and pulling at the blue angora cardigan, her pale eyes blinking rapidly. 'I must say it was a bit of a shock to hear from you after so long. I doubt if anyone remembers me as Baking Belle.'

'And it's a long time since anyone called me Dorrie Goodman,' was the retort.

'You married then?' Belle nibbled slowly.

'I had my chances but there was only ever one man in my life and we both know what happened to him,' said the visitor, tearing into her scone with relish.

'That was a long time ago, dear, fifty years ago,' was the reply.

'So what happened to the Flight Lieutenant, the Aussie?'

'One of those wartime flings, it would never have worked out!'

'What a shame.' Dorrie sipped her tea and waited. Belle picked on her scone and waited. 'Very nice set up here, peaceful.'

'And you?'

'Oh, just a flat off the Finchley Road, very convenient though. I went on the stage, did quite well for a while.'

'Musicals?' asked the hostess politely.

'No, no . . . I was Cassie Starr, Variety, panto – that sort of thing. Getting into E.N.S.A. in the war gave me the intro . . . I wrote to you all. I don't suppose you got my mail . . . I never got a reply. We were all so busy. After the war I went on tour . . . you lose touch . . . that's how it goes. Sol never came back to Lichfield. Poor Wyn – she had her eye on him.'

'She's a grandma ten times over, lives in Tamworth or thereabouts. So you kept in touch with your mother?'

'A bit, but only after Father died. She always kept herself apart from neighbours and disapproved of me being on the stage. I don't suppose she told a soul about my broadcasts, did she?' Dorrie stared squarely in Belle's direction, watching a rose flush suffuse across her cheekbones, her eyes evasive under this powerful scrutiny. The intense gaze then roamed across the oak dresser, as if looking for something to be there. Belle glanced briefly in the same direction.

'You put away all the wedding photos, then? And Victy's Graduation Day? The playgroup snaps of Charlie and Sam. They must be at university by now!'

Belle splutters, spilling tea on her skirt. 'You know about Victy?' she gasps.

'Of course I bloody well do, woman. Of course I know about your child, my daughter. Why do you think I've come back, after all this time? Come to put a stop to this stupid charade you've had us all play for years. How could you . . . How could YOU, of all people, do this to me? . . . I always had you down as fair. Half my life, I had to carry the guilt of thinking my neglect and shame killed my newborn baby. For years I punished myself and denied myself the chance of happiness, strangled love affairs at birth, in case my secret was found out.

'Have you any idea what it is like for us unmarried mothers to hide aching breasts, cover our tracks, sniff other women's offspring with envy. How can you live with what you did to me? You bonded with my child so tightly, wrapped her in your love blanket and made her your own. She was my flesh and Lucky's. All there was left for me. Go on admit it, Belle Morton, Justice of the Peace. Hah!' Dorrie wiped the tears from her eyes and took a deep breath.

'Dorrie, I swear to God!'

'Don't call me that name. I've been Cassie for years. Dorrie was buried in my kitbag on Euston Station, the night I arrived in London, clutching your money . . . Did you know then?'

'No. No . . . You've got it all wrong. Please believe me. If you had told me the whole story, do you honestly think I would have let you walk out of the Vic? I did what I did from the best of motives, honestly. I meddled and searched, secretly on your behalf, but you just stayed away too long.'

'And just whose fault was that? You knew that one word and I'd have grown bleedin' wings, flown across oceans, to see my baby. Do you think I enjoyed being Cassie Starr, soubrette, Principal Boy, heaving trunks across draughty stations every Sunday morning? It was a novelty at first, singing for my supper, all spangles under the spotlights, but dreams built on defiance never last. Tin Pan Alley takes few prisoners when you're fair, fat and forty. I was never in the Vera Lynn league. After the Beatles hit town, it was back to the kitchen for Cinderella. Back where I first began!'

Belle bowed her head. 'I'm sorry. All this time you knew and Victy too. Who told her?'

'Who do you think fed her on stories of chocolate drummer boys and fairies, dancing in the Victory Café?'

'I sent the Prin away.'

'Not far enough, Mrs Morton. Your daughter, my child, was told stories by the pixie lady in the park, who used to give her sweets and tell the little girl how she was really her own fairy godmother, the one who had once rescued her; how one day, her real princess mummy on the wireless would collect her and take her back to a palace in London.'

'Oh! No!' Isobel cried.

Dorrie ignored her. 'The Princess never came and she thought her mother didn't care. She thought if she was a

236

good girl and kept this secret, then the poor pixie woman would not be taken away to the dark dungeons and punished by a wicked policeman. That's what secrets do, Belle Morton, distort, disfigure and dishonour us all! Our generation is so good at keeping secrets, skilled in the ancient art by generations of well-meaning women. Did you ever sing a hymn in Sunday school, "Jesus bids us shine with a pure clear light, Like a little candle burning in the night"? I was taught to snuff out the light. What is hidden is for the best. Now, they don't give a toss for shameful secrets. You can pay bills with secrets; the currency of our times.

'Why did you rob me of the chance to choose? Ignorance is not bliss; it is just not knowing your options. Now I can only be an onlooker, grateful for what Victy will share with me of her past. Thank God the truth usually comes out. You silenced the Prin with threats but you did not silence the child's curiosity or her anger!'

'Is she very angry with me?'

'Ask her yourself! Victy was curious, poor girl, so she asked around. Wyn and Maggie told her bits, enough to trace herself back to the Cottage Homes and the stories of her arrival tallied. She heard about the postcard from Dorrie Daydream and she searched the E.N.S.A. records and photographs. Finally she approached the Sally Army Missing Persons Bureau. From girl to woman, it was done slowly over years, always fearful of your negative response or mine.'

'I see.'

'No, you don't see. Can you imagine WHAT it feels like to hear a voice on the end of a phone saying a forty-year-old woman wishes to contact you, a woman who thinks you may be her mother? I did bear a child but she died, I said. That's what you were told, but it may not be the case, they said. All these years of secrecy and one word from you could have sorted the matter.'

'She never asked me.' Belle folded her arms across her chest.

'Come on, woman. She was loyal and believed Santa Claus chose her for you; delivered her in his Christmas sack. Stop deceiving yourself. There was never a right time to disclose her need for identity to you. It must have been hell being half and half, after the war. No private school ever protected her from playground prejudice. It is hard for any kid to be different . . . she's a credit to herself, not us.'

'So you met then?' whispers the old woman, shrinking into the sofa.

'Not at first. We wrote and talked on the phone, got used to the sound of each other, exchanged photographs and then agreed to meet.'

'In Lichfield?'

'Oh no! I took her to see her father. In the Military Cemetery outside Cambridge, the special one for American Servicemen. We put red roses on Lucky's grave and I told her our story. We both cried. Victy said we were just like Romeo and Juliet. She brought photos of Sam and Charlie. How strange that of all the names in the world she chose her own father's for her son.'

'What did you think of her, that first time?'

'It was not the first time I had seen her. I once stopped in the Casa Blanca. I bet that scared you.'

'Yes, she told me about the red-haired woman who asked about the Victory Café, I thought you might have seen her.'

'Only a glimpse of a beautiful young Spanish woman. Lucky's mother was from Puerto Rico but I had no reason to connect them. Now she has some history for herself.'

Belle rose from her seat, pacing the floor. 'You've met them all and visited them?'

Dorrie smiled. 'Why should she not have her own secrets? Secrets in the family! Isn't that what screws up most of us, one way or the other?'

'Does she know you are here?'

'What do you think?'

'So you cooked up this visit between the two of you, to pay me back?'

'What! High Noon in the Close, rolling pins at dawn!' Dorrie burst into laughter.

Belle sank onto the arm of her chair, covering her face with wrinkled hands. 'I nearly ended it all last night, I was afraid to face you.'

'But you didn't go through with it. You were just curious enough to hang on, to see if you had got away with it all. Hid the photos though, just in case I might recognise Lucky's smile in Victy's grin. I bet you would have taken your secret to the grave.'

Belle looked up, 'Why not? That's what many women do!'

Dorrie leaned forward quickly. 'A real mother wants what's best for her child, no matter what the cost is to herself. How could you hide away a child's birthright in your selfish silence?'

'What I did, I did for love!' replied Belle with a sigh.

'Rubbish! What you did, you did for yourself. Once Digger went, she was all you had, so you clung on tight. The café was never enough. You sacrificed your own chance of a child by stealing mine. You wanted Victy all to yourself. It wasn't fair, Belle, especially to her. We both let her down.'

'What will I say to her . . . will she forgive me?'

'Can you forgive yourself for what you've done?'

'Don't worry. I'll not be staying around long enough to trouble you all.' Belle sniffed into a lace-edged handkerchief.

'There you go again, feeling sorry for yourself. I should be the Opera Queen in this scene, not you, lady! You look as tough as old leather to me. You are going to have to face her yourself and tell her your version. No deathbed confessions, madam. There's been enough colluding going on to last several lifetimes.

'She is fifty in two weeks. Life is too short for us both now to make scenes for her. Get used to the idea of sharing her around a bit. She's been handling her two mums for years and it's strained her loyalties enough. It is time to help her along. Don't go all mopey on her.

'Me and you are two old mares hitched to the same wagon now; creaky in the shanks but enough meat on the bones to pull together for a while longer. If I can come here seeking a cold revenge, wanting to see you squirm and still feel we can pull together, surely you can sort out your own mess – or you are not the Belle Morton I remember from the old days. The one who saw off that old battle tank – what was her name?'

'Connie Spear.'

'See, you do remember!'

They smiled at each other tentatively and then fell silent. A log splattered on the hearth. Belle poked the fire and set up the brass guard across the flame. She looked up. 'Do you fancy a sherry in the Angel Croft Hotel? You're right, I have to . . . we have to make this birthday special for her.'

'It will be, if we both turn up together! A bleeding miracle!'

They rose slowly, sorting out coats, gloves, scarves and boots. Outside, they linked arms, for the autumn leaves on wet cobblestones were treacherous to old bones, and night was falling fast.

RECIPES

Woolton Pie

750g (1 ½ lb) vegetables in season (carrot,
swede, turnip, leek, cauliflower)
salt
1 tablespoon vegetable extract
25g (1oz) oatmeal
1 tablespoon chopped parsley, or herb of choice

<u>Potato pastry crust</u>
50g (2oz) cooked potato, mashed
25g (1oz) available fat
50g (2oz) cheese, grated
50g (2oz) oatmeal
100g (4oz) national flour

Oven: 325°F (170°C) Gas Mark 3.

1. Peel and prepare the vegetables as appropriate, then dice. Cook
in salted water to cover, about 600ml (1 pint), until nearly tender.

2. Strain, and reserve 450ml (¾ pint) of the stock water.

3. Arrange the vegetable dice in a large pie dish.

4. Add the vegetable extract and oatmeal to the retained liquid
stock, and cook gently, stirring, until thick.

5. Pour the sauce over the vegetables, then stir in the chopped herb.

6. For the potato pastry crust, cream together the mashed potato
and fat. Add the cheese, oatmeal and flour, and mix to a stiff dough.
Rest for a few minutes in a cool place.

7. Roll out to the required size, and place over the pie dish. Bake in
the moderate oven for 30 minutes.

Bunny to the Rescue! (Jugged Hare)

SERVES 4–6

1 hare, prepared and jointed
75g (3oz) butter, margarine or available fat
600ml (1 pint) stock
1 onion, peeled and stuck with a few cloves
a bunch of local herbs (bay, thyme, etc.)
salt, pepper and cayenne pepper
25g (1oz) national flour
150ml (¼ pint) country wine or stout

Oven: 325°F (170°C) Gas Mark 3.

1. Heat 50g (2oz) of the fat and fry the hare joints on all sides.

2. Meanwhile heat the stock in a fireproof and ovenproof dish.
Drain the joints and put into the stock with the onion, herbs and
seasonings.

3. Cover and cook in the slow oven until tender, about 3–4 hours.

4. Half an hour before serving, mix the remaining fat and the flour
together, and add to the dish to thicken it.

5. Add the wine or stout, and stew gently for a further 10–15
minutes.

Serve with game chips and redcurrant or rowanberry jelly.

Brownies

8 PORTIONS

75g (3oz) self-raising flour
225g (8oz) Demerara sugar
40g (1½oz) cocoa powder
100g (4oz) margarine or butter, melted
2 eggs
2 tablespoons milk
1 teaspoon vanilla extract
50g (2oz) broken walnuts

Oven: 350°F (180°C) Gas Mark 4.
1. Grease and line a baking tin, 28 × 18cm (11 × 7 in).
2. Put the flour and sugar into a bowl.
3. Stir the cocoa into the melted butter, and pour on to the dry ingredients. Do not stir yet.
4. Beat the eggs in a mixing bowl, then add the milk and vanilla. Stir this into the butter, flour and sugar, until you have a smooth dark brown batter. Stir in the nuts.
5. Pour the batter into the greased lined tin and bake in a moderate oven until the edges are crisp and slightly coming away from the sides of the tin, about 25–30 minutes.
6. Cool and cut into brownie fingers.

Leah Fleming

Shropshire Fidget Pie

SERVES 6

450g (1lb) potatoes
450g (1lb) apples
1 tablespoon sugar if required
225g (8oz) ham or bacon, diced
salt and pepper
150ml (¼ pint) stock, cider or beer
225g (8oz) rich shortcrust pastry, chilled and rested a little milk

Oven: 350°F (180°C) Gas Mark 4.

1. Peel and slice the potatoes thinly.

2. Peel, core and slice the apples, and sprinkle sugar over them if tart.

3. Arrange the potato, ham and apple in layers in a deep pie dish, seasoning each layer.

4. Cover with the stock.

5. Roll out the pastry, cover the pie, and decorate with trimmings. Glaze with a little milk.

6. Cook low down in a moderate oven for 1 hour.

Tea Cup Loaf

8–10 SLICES

Use a standard sized tea cup.

1 cup sultanas or ½ cup sultanas and ½ cup chopped dates

2 cups cold strong tea

2 cups self-raising flour

½ cup brown sugar

I dessertspoon dark treacle (warmed first in the tin)

enough milk to soften the dough

Oven: 325°F (170°C) Gas Mark 3.

1. Soak the sultanas, or sultanas and chopped dates, overnight in the cold tea. Strain any surplus tea.

2. Mix the flour, soaked fruit and sugar together.

3. Add the warmed treacle with a little milk, and mix together.

4. Grease a loaf tin well and put in the mixture.

5. Bake in the lower part of a moderate oven for about 1½ hours.

Welcome Home! Pudding

SERVES 6

750g (1½ lb) fresh fruits (raspberries, redcurrants, halved
plums, blackcurrants, chopped apples etc.) or 450g (1lb)
sliced rhubarb and 50g (2oz) soaked prunes
300ml (½ pint) water
225g (8oz) sliced bread
50g (2oz) sugar

1. Stew the fruit gently in the water until tender.
2. Grease a pudding basin, and line the bottom and sides with
triangles of sliced bread, keeping the trimmings for the middle
layers.
3. Strain the juice from the fruit pulp, and soak the bread in the
basin thoroughly with most of it.
4. Fill the basin with alternate layers of bread, fruit and sugar. Finish
with a layer of bread on top. Pack it very tightly, then pour the
remaining juice over the bread cover.
5. Weight the top with a saucer and weight, and leave to chill
overnight.
6. Ease the pudding away from the sides of the basin gently, then
turn out onto a deep plate. Cover with any remaining juices.

Garnish with mint leaves and berries, and serve with cream.

Bortsch

SERVES 4

25g (1oz) dripping or margarine
1 large beetroot, peeled and grated
2 potatoes, peeled and grated
1 large carrot, peeled and grated
1 onion, peeled and grated
350g (12oz) cabbage, very finely shredded
1 stick celery, grated
1 large bunch of fresh herbs in season (parsley,
marjoram, bay leaf), plus a few cloves
stock (preferably made from the remains of poultry carcasses)

1. Melt the dripping in a large pan and fry the beetroot for 5 minutes.
2. Add all the other vegetables to the beetroot, along with the herbs and cloves, and cover with good stock.
3. Bring to the boil. Remove any scum.
4. Put on the lid, and simmer slowly for 2 hours. Pick out the herbs and cloves, then liquidise or leave chunky.

To serve, add a whirl of soured cream and a sprinkling of chopped parsley.

Spicy Sauce to Perk up a Grill

SERVES 4

2 shallots, peeled and chopped

1 tablespoon oil

2 tablespoons malt vinegar

10 peppercorns, crushed

2 tablespoons brown sauce

½ teaspoon Worcestershire sauce

½ teaspoon made-up mustard

1 tablespoon dark brown sugar

1 tablespoon tomato paste

1. Sauté the shallots in the oil until golden.
2. Add the rest of the ingredients, and simmer gently to reduce.
3. Sweeten further to taste.

Serve with grilled meat or sausages.

Victory Pie

SERVES 4–6

225g (8oz) haricot beans, soaked in water overnight and drained

600ml (1 pint) water

1 tablespoon dripping

1 onion, peeled and chopped

1 cm (½ in) fresh root ginger bruised, or

2 teaspoons powdered ginger

225g (8oz) ham, bacon or pork if available, diced

1 large cooking apple, cored and sliced

1 teaspoon made-up mustard

1 tablespoon molasses (black treacle will do) salt and pepper

<u>Pie topping</u>

50g (2oz) breadcrumbs

50g (2oz) national flour

50g (2oz) oatmeal

100g (4oz) margarine

a little grated cheese and dried mixed herbs to garnish

Oven: 350°F (180°C) Gas Mark 4.

1. Cook the beans in the water for about one and a half hours. Drain and reserve some of the stock.

2. Heat the fat in a pan and lightly fry the onion, ginger, meat, and finally apple.

3. Place in a pie dish with the mustard, molasses and a little of the reserved stock. Season to taste with salt and pepper.

4. Blend together the breadcrumbs, flour, oatmeal and margarine in a bowl to a crumble texture, and firm over the top of the pie.

5. Sprinkle with grated cheese and dried herbs. Place in the bottom of a moderate oven and bake for 1 hour.

Elderflower Champagne

ENOUGH FOR 4 WINE BOTTLES

Juice and grated rind of 2 precious lemons
4 fresh elderflower heads, pick on a dry day
2 tablespoons white vinegar
600g (1 ¼ lb) white sugar
4 generous litres (1 gallon) water

1. Place all the ingredients in a large bowl, and leave, covered, for 24 hours.
2. Strain and bottle.
3. Leave for at least two weeks before drinking, but not for too long, or it will serve as a hand grenade!

Belle's Utility Christmas Pudding 1944 (no fat!)

SERVES 6

750g (1½ lb) available dried fruit (figs,
prunes, dates, sultanas, raisins etc)
stout, rum or brandy
175g (6oz) national flour
a pinch of salt
1 teaspoon mixed spice
100g (4oz) breadcrumbs
2 tablespoons dark treacle (warmed first in the tin) grated
peel of 1 orange and lemon, plus the juice if possible
3 eggs, beaten, or equivalent reconstituted egg
150ml (¼ pint) milk
150ml (¼ pint) stout or cider
225g (8oz) carrots, peeled and grated

1. Soak the dried fruit overnight in enough stout, rum or brandy to cover. Use any not absorbed in the pudding.
2. Mix the dry ingredients into the bowl of soaked dried fruit.
3. Add the warmed treacle, citrus rind and juice, beaten eggs, milk and stout.
4. Add the grated carrot, stir up, and make a wish!
5. Put into a greased 1.4 litre (two and a half pint) pudding basin, and cover with greased butter paper and muslin. Seal tightly.
6. Steam in a pan of water, covered for 6 hours. Keep checking the water level, topping up if necessary!
7. Cool and store.
8. Steam for a further 2½ hours before serving.

Serve with white sauce flavoured with brandy essence.

Leah Fleming

Spam Fritters

SERVES 4

50g (2oz) national flour
a pinch of salt
1 egg yolk, or equivalent reconstituted egg
1.2 litres (2 pints) milk, or milk and water
a pinch of dried mixed herbs
1 teaspoon grated onion
1 teaspoon chopped parsley
175g (6oz) spam, thinly chopped
25g (1oz) cooking fat

1. Mix together the flour, salt, egg and liquid.
2. Beat until a smooth batter, then add the herbs, onion, parsley and spam.
3. Heat a frying pan, melt the fat, and drop in spoonfuls of the mixture.
4. Fry quickly on each side until crisp and brown, and serve immediately or else!

Yorkshire 'Cheese' Tarts

SERVES 12

Pastry

350g (12oz) national flour
175g (6oz) soft margarine
50g (2oz) caster sugar

Filling

75g (3oz) sugar
100g (4oz) margarine
2 tablespoons desiccated coconut
75g (3oz) currants
1 egg, beaten

Oven: 325°F (170°C) Gas Mark 3.

1. Work together the flour, fat and sugar for the pastry.

2. Add enough cold water to make a soft but not sticky dough.

3. Cover and chill in the fridge for 10 minutes.

4. Roll out and cut into suitable sized rounds. Line greased pastry tins with the pastry rounds, and chill again.

5. For the filling, beat together the sugar and fat, then add all the remaining filling ingredients. Mix to a paste.

6. Spoon into each pastry case, place in the middle of a moderate oven, and bake until golden, about 20 minutes.

Celebration Pudding

Serves 6

8 tablespoons drinking chocolate powder
2 tablespoons coffee or cocoa powder
100g (4oz) grated breadcrumbs
100g (4oz) Demerara sugar (but any will do!)

Filling

450ml (¾ pint) double cream (mock cream substitute will do)
50g (2oz) grated chocolate or vermicelli

1. Mix the dry ingredients together in a bowl.
2. Beat the cream until fluffy.
3. Put a layer of dry mixture in the bottom of a glass bowl. Top with some cream, then alternate layers, light then dark. Finish with a chocolate layer.
4. Sprinkle over with the topping of your choice.
5. Chill, and let stand if you can!

Isobel's Scone Recipe

8 PORTIONS

100g (4oz) self-raising flour
100g (4oz) wholemeal self-raising flour
1 teaspoon baking powder
50g (2oz) soft margarine
25g (1oz) caster sugar
1 egg
150ml (¼ pint milk)

Oven: 425°F (220°C) Gas Mark 7.

1. Sieve the flours and baking powder into a bowl, then rub in the fat until the mixture resembles breadcrumbs.

2. Mix in the sugar, then gradually add the egg, beaten with the milk, to make a good dough. Leave a little egg mixture over for the glaze.

3. Turn out onto a floured board and knead gently. Shape and roll into a square.

4. Dip a 2-inch cutter in some extra flour and cut out about eight thick scones.

5. Brush the tops with the last of the egg and milk mixture.

6. Place on a greased baking sheet and bake at the top of a hot oven. Inspect after 10 minutes. Place on a rack to cool before eating.

Turn the page to read *The Recipe*,
an exclusive short story by Leah Fleming

THE RECIPE

It was a truth universally acknowledged in the village that Epiphany Birkett, or Fanny, as she was known, was the undisputed Queen of Cakes, the Mary Berry of Wintergill. Her recipes appeared in the *Dalesman*, but it was her Christmas cake recipe, handed down for generations, that was a secret never to be told. No one knew what secret ingredients or exact proportions made her cakes better than all the rest.

There was always a rush to buy a ticket to guess the weight of the beautiful iced offering she gave to the Christmas Bazaar. In fact, for the Summer Show, they made her a judge so that all of the other contestants would have a chance of winning rosettes in the bake-off. All of this was told to me many times over coffee after our family arrived in the village. We had just finished renovating the old farmhouse at the end of a lane, and rumour was that we had won the lottery, judging by the size of our four-by-four that contained two kids and a large dog, and by the fact we'd come from 'down south'.

Yet one by one, our neighbours kindly trooped to the door with gifts of eggs and offers of help with the garden. They all wanted a peep at what we'd done to Elsie Crummock's old house, especially at the kitchen alterations which were still only half finished. 'If you are going to compete in the culinary stakes, you better resign yourself to defeat. Oh, I tell a lie! Fanny will actually be the judge this year for the Christmas Cake bake-off,' said Sally, my neighbour from next door.

I nodded, thinking that baking cakes wasn't high on my list of priorities. In fact, I was dreading the coming festive season. 'She'll get nothing from me,' I smiled. 'I'm too busy with the house.'

'But it's for a good cause,' Sally insisted. 'It's to support Crisis at Christmas and to make sure the homeless get a roof over their heads. Just because we live in the sticks doesn't mean we don't care.'

'I know, I'm sorry, it's just I've got a lot on.' How could I explain to a stranger how low I was feeling, how tired I was? And that just keeping the family fed and watered while they settled into new schools and jobs was such an effort of will?

My husband, Guy, thought the move would ease the pain; a move away from familiar haunts and memories. And it was such a beautiful village, with plenty of space for Ellie and Patrick to play. It was perfect except for the one thing that was missing.

I felt my stomach tighten. It was flat: I had shrunk in the effort to join in and be friendly. And Sally was nosey in a nice way, her eyes darting round the smart worktops and surfaces with curiosity. 'Old Elsie wouldn't know her place, it's so modern and warm with the Aga. I can remember these walls dripping with treacle nicotine. Her boys were great smokers. Still, I expect it's strange coming from a city. Where did you say it were?'

I didn't. I wish you'd go home, I thought, rising to clear the cups as a hint. 'Goodness, is that the time?'

'And here's me blethering on. Can we count on you for a cake to be auctioned off?' Sally was not going to let me off the hook. I nodded wearily, despite the fact that I'd never baked a Christmas cake in my life. We bought one ready-iced from a good bakery. Why was it in the country you were expected to make your own? And for it to be judged and sold with fancy icing: oh, what the hell had I let myself in for? And who was this Fanny? Somebody from the big house, lady of the manor? That's all I needed. Well, she'll get short shrift if she ever comes to call, I sighed to myself.

The whole idea slipped from my cluttered mind until the woman in the post office pointed to the bake-off poster next to a whole shelf of ingredients: soft brown sugar, mixed peel, glace cherries and cake frills. 'I always do mine at half-term,' she suggested, as I tried to ignore the shelf. 'It gives it a chance to mature and I feed it brandy every week to keep it moist. Do you have a special recipe?' I shook my head. 'A book of first-class stamps, please.' Here we go again, I thought. Have they nothing better to do than make cake?

'Everyone would love to get their hands on Epiphany's secret recipe that has passed from mother to daughter for a hundred years. There's such richness to the texture and you can smell the alcohol before it's even cut. Have you met her yet?'

'Does she own this village, then?' I asked, a bit sharply.

'Oh, not at all, she just has the knack of getting everyone involved. Enthusiastic is the word for Fanny! Good luck with your cake: the earlier it's done, the better it tastes.'

I wondered how on earth was I supposed to fiddle with cakes when I had a half-term house full of noisy kids and cousins? The thought of Christmas to come was the last thing on my mind. If only I didn't feel so exhausted. 'I'm not sure this was a good move,' I complained to Guy one night.

'Give it time, Charley, grief has its own rhythm.'

'But it should have been such a wonderful Christmas. We were so looking forward to . . .' The tears started again, as they had done for months now.

'The doctors said to expect this,' Guy reminded me. 'Your hormones are all over the show. Don't worry, you don't have to do anything you don't want to.'

'But we chose a village to be part of its life. I don't want to seem standoffish but I don't want to bake some sodden apology for a cake. We'll give a donation instead.' But I knew this was giving up again, taking the easy option. I could hear my mother's challenge in my ears: 'If you don't try, you'll never know'.

So, the following week, I roamed the local supermarket shelves with a list from a Googled recipe, looking for eggs (free range, of course), and flour – but which one? Oh hell! I found myself muttering out loud next to a woman, who turned and smiled.

'Is it for a Christmas cake?'

'Not any old cake but one for the bake-off at Wintergill. I haven't a clue what I am doing. This recipe is off the Internet but I've got an Aga . . .'

The woman was wearing a jazzy puffa jacket and had silvery blue hair. 'Let me look? Hmm, it's a bit Spartan. This your first attempt?'

I laughed. 'Can't you tell? Still, it's all for a good cause, so I'm giving it a go. I wish it was brownies. I can churn them out by the dozen.'

'Are you new to the area?'

'Yes, moved into Wintergill a few months ago. Are you local?' I asked.

'Oh yes, born and bred. It's a lovely village and young people with families coming in are always a bonus. Holiday homes can kill the life out some places, but not Wintergill.'

We parted company at the check-out, and that was that until the next morning, when the front door bell rang. The woman from the shop was standing on my doorstep, large as life, holding a beautiful sponge cake. And there I was: mop in hand, with Velcro rollers stuck in my hair.

'I wondered if it was you!' she exclaimed. 'I'm sorry it has taken me so long to call in. Epiphany Birkett, from across the green.' She walked right into the hallway, avoiding the bucket and the jumping dog.

'Do come in, please. I'm Charlotte Foley but everyone calls me Charley. Can I offer you a coffee?' I asked, as I led the way to the kitchen.

'That would be lovely, thanks. And everyone calls me Fanny behind my back. I gather the Christmas bake-off is causing you some concern?'

'It's not that I'm not willing, but I've never baked big cakes before. Rice Krispy bakes and casseroles I can do, but I haven't the time or inclination to tackle anything more complicated.' There was an edge to my voice that I couldn't hide. 'I didn't expect to be corralled into this bake-off thing and it's not my forte. Sorry to let you all down, but I'll give you a donation instead.'

'What is it about baking you can't do?' Fanny was looking at me with interest and concern.

'It the whole flipping business; all the Christmas must-do mullarkey. Doing cards is bad enough.' To my horror, tears began again as I tried to pour the coffee with trembling hands.

'Let me do that.' Fanny took over. 'You've moved here, which is stressful enough, and done an excellent makeover of Elsie's farmhouse – another stress – and along comes the annual Christmas preparations. I remember when my children were young I used to dread it. Making the perfect Christmas is not achievable. It's a rotten myth. But there's something else troubling you, isn't there?'

I looked up through my tears. 'It should have been a wonderful time. We were looking forward to a new life. Everything was perfect until three months ago, when the scan showed no life, nothing. He should have been our Christmas baby born in the village. I still can't believe it. We were going to call him Noel. I'm sorry, I . . .'

'Why should you apologise for losing a precious child? It tears the guts out of you to lose a little one, especially in that way.'

'You too?' I asked, sensing her meaning. I watched as she swallowed back the tears.

'Mary was born "asleep", as they say now. Perfect in every way. She would have been our only girl. I have sons, but you never forget the loss, never, ever . . . We all grieve in our own way, though, and I see baking, which was such a comfort to me, is not for you. I do understand.'

'If only I felt I could do it and not make a fool of myself,' I said. 'We have to have a Christmas cake.'

'You just follow the instructions, step by step. Take the time to soak your fruit, and use the best you can afford. I have a recipe that is tried and tested and you are welcome to use it, my dear. It has never failed.'

'That's very kind, but that's your secret recipe,' I blurted out.

She laughed. 'Ah ha, the jungle drums have been beating?'

'Epiphany's Christmas cake is a great legend. The holy grail of Christmas baking, or so I am told.' I found I was smiling.

'And the secret ingredient is some mysterious elixir of spices, a hocus-pocus spell performed with smells and bells. Is that what they think?' Fanny burst out laughing. 'If only they knew.'

I held my breath, waiting for this unexpected and welcome revelation, but Fanny just sipped her coffee slowly, smiling. Her dark eyes flashed with mischief. 'Shall I tell you what my most magical ingredient is: the one passed down from generation to generation? It is such a simple one, Charlotte. It's just love. If you give something or someone time and love, you'll be surprised at the result. We have an old Yorkshire saying to go with it: "A cake without cheese is like a kiss without a squeeze". So put on your favourite music, gather everything together, measure out carefully and cook it all slowly. Remember, with time and love, nothing is impossible.'